The Origins of Misgiving

Robert Froese

Flat Bay Press

Flat Bay Press
P.O. Box 217
Harrington, Maine 04643

Copyright © 2009 by Robert Froese
All rights reserved

ISBN-10: 0-9715382-3-9
ISBN-13: 978-0-9715382-3-8

This is a work of fiction. All incidents, names, and characters are either imaginary or are used fictitiously. Any resemblance of these characters to actual persons, living or dead, is entirely coincidental.

Printed on recycled paper.

For Flat Bay Collective---
Leonore Hildebrandt, Dick Miles, Susan Hammond,
Donna Kausen, Bernie Vinzani,
Tony Brinkley, and Brian Stewart

The ocean is theirs now,
the vacancy, freezing and burning,
the solitude crowded with bonfires.

-- Pablo Neruda, "Old Women by the Sea"

The Origins of Misgiving

THE SKY is holding flat above the wet pavement ahead, the two opposing slices of identical gray. The sides of the highway bulge with green. The trees, the hedges, the lawns together devour whatever trash there is. Any more green and the scene would explode. I'm keeping just over the speed limit. I'm not in a hurry to be anywhere. The tires hiss, spraying water. I'm trying now to take all of this in, trying to pay attention. Gradually the windshield blurs. Then suddenly, silently, the wipers sweep it clear, making the scene new again.

Not that any of this is really new. For the sake of novelty, I'd be better off driving with my eyes closed, alert for the blare of a car horn. And, at some point, the impact. That would be new, not this. The familiar at times can lull a person to sleep. Memory bleeds into life. It's hard to know where you are, or when. Today, I'm trying to prevent that from happening, but it is a struggle. The heroic, these days, comes down to this.

For the moment traffic is light, not as inevitable as at rush hour. Right now, I might turn off down one of these roads. Or not. It's entirely up to me. I could end up almost anywhere, wild as that idea seems.

I come up behind a car, a minivan crawling, obstructing my view of the road ahead. Gradually my windshield grimes over. Not a problem, though. As soon as the way is clear, I pull out and pass. The acceleration presses me into the seat. My foot on the gas, the oncoming lane is open ahead as far as I can see. I am a free man—that's the way it feels.

These other drivers—who knows where they're headed? The post office, the dry cleaners, the Jiffy-Lube. Most of the faces behind the windshields, I can't help noticing, belong to women. There is no practical significance in this. I don't know any of the women. But—God, yes—their faces are a blessing. Angelic, entirely selfless at this distance, they are not asking for anything. For each face, I imagine an entire woman seated—in abstract, somewhat ideal form—behind the wheel. Her imaginary limbs stretch and flex against undergarments, usually a gray skirt, some pastel blouse or other. It is possible. The truth is I have no idea what these women are wearing, much less why they are out at this hour, scouting the neighborhood from behind their windshields. My ignorance, where women are concerned, is considerable.

The air hangs over the highway, strangely thick. Ordinarily, I wouldn't notice the air. Entire weeks go by—I hardly know it's there. Today it seems there's no getting around it. This drizzle, it's enough to make me wonder whether, beyond what I can see, there actually is a world out there. The wipers seem a bit sluggish, so I adjust them. Running over a rougher patch of road, I hear a rattling behind me. Probably my clubs in the trunk of the car, an almost complete set of Callaways. I don't have a lot to say about those. Another rough patch, and I hear them again.

Fifty-seven miles per hour or not, my mind arrives at a standstill. The fact is I'm not sure why I'm doing this, taking off early from work. I've never done it before. Maybe I need to catch my breath. Or maybe something else. But I find there's a feeling that goes along with it—as though I'm entering new and possibly dangerous territory. I wonder how it will sit with Brenda.

But now all at once I come upon a road jutting off to the left, climbing steeply away from the highway and out of the woods. Over the trees I get a glimpse of it cutting through higher meadow until it is obscured by mist. I have never seen this road before. It surprises me. Not the road itself, but the fact that it could have been there, presumably for years, without my ever noticing. I don't seriously consider taking the road. Frankly, something about it scares me.

The highway sweeps right, then left again. Good. This is as it should be. The car adheres to the eastbound lane, never once touching the centerline. Unsuspected muscles in my arms and hands, I imagine, are responsible for this. I concentrate, trying to picture how they do it, and immediately my driving becomes sloppy, erratic. As if muscles don't like their privacy invaded.

I pass the University—so many red bricks!—its campus sprawling up the hill into fog. Then, a mile further, the busy entrance to the Mall. The buildings, the lawns, the signs—I'm seeing the things I see every day, only maybe this time a fraction too late, as if whatever could happen already has. At the intersection by the Mobil station, I signal and turn left as usual. But another half, three-quarters of a mile and I am caught by a sudden impulse. I pull over to the side of the road and turn the engine off. I roll my window partway down and sit.

I watch and listen.

There, it's happened again. I don't know what it is. A general softening in the outlines of things. Some subtle lift to the terrain. The restraint in vegetation that comes with pruning and landscaping. Or maybe something in the background sound. A less vulgar population of insects. Whatever it is, there's no mistaking the transition. I have entered the vicinity of Brandewoode. Though I can't see more than a couple of hundred feet, I'm aware of the land rolling away in all directions like an ocean whose violence is, for the moment, frozen. Earlier I heard on the news: hurricane season has officially begun. Sitting in my car, I feel swallowed, as though in the trough of a great wave. I roll the window down another few inches. Then all the way.

This drizzle. I'm trying to remember when it began.

The Faces of Women

THE CALL of a nearby thrush interrupts the damp air. We see nothing of the bird—its call might be intrinsic, a sound concocted by the moment itself. Despite the mist and overcast, there is a heavy lucidity to the scene in front of the house. The rhododendrons and azaleas are in flower. Their blossoms flare against the dark of the woods, and the lawn glows all the more brightly for lack of sun. Each tree has acquired its own space. Something is at work here. There is about the grounds an impression of permanence, the deliberate illusion of stillness.

The air waits. The bird sings again. And now movement at the foot of the long driveway. The car appears as if materializing out of nothing rather than arriving from some other place. Metallic gray, it advances over the pavement, noiseless as a shadow.

The scene remains (as far as we can tell) unaffected by this intrusion, except perhaps for a flutter of darkening about one of the windows, making it appear oddly as if the house were composing itself, shrugging off the sting of this small inconvenience.

The car continues its approach around the sloping lawn, past the red maple, the dogwood and wisteria. Finally, near the flagstone walk leading to the front door, its tires roll to a stop upon the blacktop. For a moment it simply sits there in photographic motionlessness. The woods, the lawn, the house, the car—a picture of equilibrium, reflected, we could imagine, in the regardful eye of the thrush.

All at once the car door swings open, releasing into the drizzly air the thin chime of an alarm. For a moment, one foot on the pavement, the driver pauses as though stalled in a confusion between inside and outside. Until at last he pulls the key from the ignition, restoring what feels like silence, but not the same silence. He emerges from the car and stands in the driveway, gazing up at the house. For several moments he remains like this, making no move. There is no way of telling whether he intends to approach and enter the house or whether he is content contemplating it from this distance.

    Now at an upstairs window a curtain is pushed aside, and a woman holds her face to the glass. She stares down at him, her face perfectly expressionless. The thrush calls again. The driver narrows his eyes. After a moment the curtain falls back into place and the face disappears. The driver stands another moment before suddenly turning and looking back along the driveway, as if only now aware of being watched.

AS FAR AS I can see, there is no color at all. Even staring hard at something I know to be red, or blue, the best I can come up with is a kind of gummy gray not very different from the gray surrounding it. Except, of course, for the green digital readouts on the microwave and the range, but at the moment I'm trying to ignore them. One reads 1:37, the other 1:39. Either way, it's no hour to be sitting in my bathrobe on a kitchen stool. Tonight, for some reason, I haven't been able to sleep. I've had this tangible feeling that makes it hard for me to relax. I don't know how to describe it—as if something is crawling through the neighborhood. Something large and slow, inching its way forward.

The lights are all switched off. Still, the nightlights in the kitchen and the hall cast a dull illumination. And there's a sort of glow from outside, what may be the moon through the clouds. It's difficult to say. I haven't seen the moon in months. Or it might be coming from the parking lot lamps at the Mall a few miles away. Anyway, I can see well enough to sit here, sipping a glass of milk.

Normally I don't have trouble sleeping. Why should I? It's been happening only recently. Stan says my problem is an excess of happiness. Stan, who I know from work, isn't afraid to give advice. Just the other day—I forget what we were talking about—he told me I'd be better off with a little tragedy in my life. I didn't like the sound of that.

I won't deny living a blessed existence—it's embarrassing even talking about it. But it wasn't always that way. Early on, we went through some rough times, Brenda and I, which is what eventually brought us here to Brandewoode. That would have been a little over five years ago.

Brenda took charge of the move. She was ruthless when it came to the furniture. Not that there was anything wrong with our furniture. But I think she understood better than I, in coming to Brandewoode we were making a clean start. I was on the verge of putting my foot down when she left the oak diningroom table behind—stained to look like cherry. Then I saw the piece she was replacing it with—pure, unveneered walnut with matching chairs. "We'll be taking our meals at this table," she said. So that was that.

Life in the city had been wearing us down, for all the usual reasons: the noise, the pollution, the filth. Not to mention—what Brenda pointed out—the relentless, oppressive geometry. She had begun painting and was noticing these things. We were suffering, Brenda said, from "biotic starvation." She flung that phrase into the air one evening, offhandedly, as if she owned it. She'd taken up reading, too, then.

Of course she had a point. Locked in our apartment, we weren't seeing a lot of the natural world. There were the rodents and pigeons and plenty of those brownish birds that go with the urban landscape. Trees, along particular avenues, had been encouraged up out of the concrete. And indoors we still bothered to maintain the usual token house plants. But that was it.

Anyway, biotic starvation wasn't what drove us out of the city. No, even Brenda admitted, it was simple, raw fear. It surprised us, maybe even shamed us in the end, to feel that defenseless. I don't mean the reports on nightly news or the word-of-mouth accounts circulating at the time, disturbing as these were. No, I'm talking about day-to-day living. We never knew how it happened. It got to the point where we didn't dare walk to the corner store.

The neighborhood kids. Perched on window ledges like gargoyles, they kept watch incessantly. The word "kids" can't account for them. The ringleader—he couldn't have been older than twelve—wore the name STEVE tattooed across the crown of his shaved head. He'd plant himself in our way on the sidewalk and force us to walk around him. He and his underlings took over vacant buildings on the block, taunted us by name from the windows, and threw things at us you wouldn't want to touch. They stole our mail and sprinkled bits of it on us like confetti as we walked by. And it didn't end there. Cracks and fissures of geological proportions appeared in the pavement of parking lots. Cars swerved to run us over. We began noticing the taste of metal in our mouths. There was the sense—we both felt it—that something had taken over the sky. We were living like rabbits on a ship of wolves.

What surprises me now is that we lasted as long as we did. Maybe we thought somehow we deserved it, I don't know. Anyway, after who knows how many months, we decided we'd had enough.

We turned our attention north and west of the city, launching on weekend exploratory drives beyond the strips and the suburbs into what we called "the country." Forty-five minutes, we'd decided, and no further. I don't know what we were thinking. Neither of us had ventured outside the city in years. We imagined, I suppose, forgotten tracts of land, fine old houses in need of repair. It was a cruel dream. The economy, when it came to real estate, had forgotten nothing. There were no tracts of land. All those fine old houses, gobbled up and repaired long ago, were selling for seven figures now. Two hours and more out from the city, there wasn't a stitch of property we could have afforded.

On a Sunday evening after one of these drives—it must have taken us over four-hundred miles—we sat stunned at the dinner table in what back then passed for silence, the howls and maniacal laughter ascending from the streets below, signaling the advance of night. It was clear we'd exhausted every possibility. "Look," I said finally, "maybe we need to reevaluate." But I didn't know what I meant by that. Brenda just stared at the table. She didn't say anything. The room kept getting darker, but neither of us moved to turn on the light. A drizzle of fine chemical dust continued to find its way in through the windows. We could hear it.

It wasn't a week later, Brenda's grandmother died—heart attack on a flight from Seattle to Phoenix. Eighty-four years old. Brenda was away for a few days, taking care of funeral arrangements, and so on. And when she returned, I couldn't help noticing, she seemed changed. She appeared all at once older, and altogether more quietly beautiful than I had ever seen her. Moving about the apartment, she barely said a word. Still, I knew she was communicating something. I happened then to come into the bedroom while she was unpacking her suitcase. And it struck me, unmistakably, that the quality of light around her was somehow clearer, better defined, without there being any change I could put my finger on. As though there were spaces behind the walls of this room, illuminated by roving, benevolent suns. I'm not describing it right, I know, but the impression was so distinct that I was actually drawn to the window to glance out into the street, expecting to see . . . who knows what.

  She told me then. She sat down on the bed and, her hands clasped in her lap, made a simple statement of it. Her face was wonderfully expressionless. Her grandmother's estate, she said, had fallen to her. She paused, then added that it amounted to nearly . . . well, it seems wrong even mentioning the figure. It was then that I began to feel the change too. I remained standing at the window. After all, there was no reason not to. Fate had just bestowed upon me all the time in the world. My eyes wandered the sidewalks below. The menaces there seemed to present themselves now from some acceptable distance, though with a familiar glow, as if I were recognizing in that scene pieces of adventures I'd heard about secondhand. I could have stood in that position at the window, I think, indefinitely.

  So we came to Brandewoode.

  A friend had told us about it. At first we didn't quite believe him. But one look and we understood: all those months we had been searching blindly, and now our blindness was past. People call Brandewoode a development, a neighborhood, a gated community. I don't think of it in any of those ways. To begin with, none of the Brandewoode homes look new. No question, they are all tight, expertly built, and beautifully proportioned. Each occupies its own space, though, with (as one of the brochures put it) "the modest, solid magnificence that comes to architecture only with age." Each—one gets the impression—is a home with a story. There is something about the light, the way the windows catch the sun unexpectedly, as if by reflection off something fleeting and unseen. Even on cloudy days, some renegade glow seems to filter through, warming the bricks and clapboards and illuminating the rooms inside like mildly bittersweet memories.

  But forget about houses, what matters here is the landscape. It has a certain look to it—wild and cultivated and magical all at once. Like a backdrop for Arthurian legend. There is forest. I know next to nothing about trees, but I'm confident we have oak. And beech, I've heard it said. Quite a few tall evergreens. And the smaller trees—dogwood might be one—and all the undergrowth and vines. Mostly, though, it's the *way* things grow in Brandewoode, trees taking on shapes you can't ignore. "Chiaroscuro vegetation," Brenda calls it. The light and shadow suggest surprising, even disturbing depths to these woods, though really they're little more than beauty strips. Then there's all that granite everywhere—the flesh of the earth. In the woods and out on the rolling meadows and lawns, the ground thins, exposing the rock—not the jagged kind, but rounded, smooth. Feminine, Brenda said when she saw it. Standing there, the two of us gazing upon the grounds, we knew we were on the threshold of something.

Even afterward for the first few years we felt some of that lingering anxiousness, the fear that something of our past might yet pursue us, might yet hunt us down. But it didn't happen. After awhile we forgot about it. That time before Brandewoode now seems little more than a distant nightmare. And in a way I can take comfort in it, counting our past suffering as ample payment for our present happiness.

Upstairs, just now, I hear sweet Brenda sigh and turn over in her sleep. I tilt the glass and down the last of the milk. Maybe it does have a calming effect. Through the kitchen window I can see a good part of the back yard, or at least a shadowy version of it. The shrubs and trees and flower beds seem to shift and move, and when I look directly at them, they disappear altogether. I get up and put the empty milk glass in the sink. I run a little tap water in it. I don't know, maybe I can sleep now.

I T IS THURSDAY. Or maybe Wednesday. The days have a pudgy, doughy feel—they lose their edges and stick to one another. As if time didn't slice very well. Anyway here I am, stalled in the quiet of my office, fascinated—judging from the direction of my stare—by something having to do with the carpet. A sculpture of me this way, my head turned slightly, might be entitled "On the Brink of Surprise." Several minutes into this spell of inertia, I feel continually on the verge of ending it, as if the decision were mine— as if, at any moment, by an exercise of will I could reenter the current of life. But I don't. What is to prevent me from sitting here like this for weeks, or even years? Our nervous systems, I'd be willing to bet, are equipped with certain override mechanisms to prevent that sort of embarrassment. Then again, maybe not.

  I don't know what it is—lack of sleep? The work environment here at Argus . . . well, I can't complain. Day care, massage, the gym, the pool. None of which I use, granted, but it all cultivates the impression that, if there were anything I did want, it would be mine for the asking. Not to mention that the work is interesting, some would even say exciting. Computer security— a top priority these days. The thing is, I don't actually need to work. I'm not the sort of guy, though, to live off his wife's inheritance.

  Meanwhile, nagging at the edge of my vision are a couple of neon-pink Post-its that Sonya earlier stuck to my desk. I'm supposed to return two phone calls. One from Mel Pettigrew in Development. The other from Marjorie Lundstrom, Sonya's luscious handwriting informs me, ASAP. I'm reporting these from memory. My eyes are still on the carpet, which—I could be persuaded—is beginning to develop something like an aura. That exercise of will hasn't yet arrived. Who knows what the holdup is.

Concerning Marjorie Lundstrom, that fairly reliable wellspring of dissatisfaction—it's no mystery why she's calling. Fresh worms and viruses have been wriggling through, playing havoc with business over there at NewBank, where Marjorie sits as Vice President of Some Thing Or Other. It's happened before, and none of us has reason to believe that it will not happen again. Eventually I'll have to return her call. The trouble, I'll try to explain to Marjorie, lies neither with our service nor with our software but rather with NB employees, who insist on opening salacious e-mail attachments. We've been through this before, Marjorie and I. The woman has a gruff way about her, not to mention a set of vocal cords evidently in tatters. A stale tobacco odor hangs over every one of our phone conversations, though I've never encountered the woman in person and can't be sure she's a smoker. In any event, I am not looking forward to the call.

With a suddenness that makes my heart jump, Vince Marconi thrusts his head into my office, dimming the glow of the carpet.

With my hands credibly in the vicinity of the keyboard, I hope I look busy enough.

He says, "You had a chance to look at that RFP?"

I nod, which normally would indicate yes, except then I say, "This afternoon. As soon as I finish this."

He glances at his watch.

"Before I leave," I say. I shake my head, which normally would indicate no, though here, I hope, it signals an emphatic affirmative.

He casts a look down the hall, then back at me. "I'm expecting there'll be some juice in this one."

The pauses between our sentences are beginning to feel uncomfortable.

"How about this?" I stare at my calendar. "I could arrange a meeting tomorrow." I'm about to add, "before the weekend," but I'm still confused on the day of the week. I leave it alone.

Vince stands now with his head cocked back, as though drawing on some reservoir of inner toughness. He is not a tall man. Here at Argus he's been a bit like a father to me, though resorting at times to severity. Relaxation, according to Vince's way of thinking, is a luxury reserved for the dead. Vince is a regular tiger. I'm lucky to have him pulling for me.

"DOD contract, Michael." He rubs his thumb back and forth against his fingers. "You know what I'm saying?"

I shake my head solemnly. "Absolutely. Absolutely."

Standing, with his hand on the doorjamb, he glances around my office. He blinks. It's hard to judge from his expression, whether he likes what he sees. His eyes come to rest on the window, which is, on this drizzly afternoon, just another rectangle of gray. Finally he nods, a fatherly nod. "Righto, Michael," he says. He gives the doorjamb a playful slap.

And he's gone, just like that. My office, as if coming to grips with his absence, turns heavily quiet. Sometimes these four walls, this ceiling and floor, the carpet, the furniture, and everything else contained here—flimsily constructed as it all is—exerts a surprising gravity. Entering in the morning and leaving every evening, especially then I feel it, pulling. I don't have an explanation for it.

Now I hear a noise at the window. What it might be, I don't know. I look, but there is nothing. Nothing but the same old field of gray, bespeckled with beads of moisture on the glass.

It wasn't so long ago I could stand at that window, gazing out over the buildings and the treetops, and take in a sweeping view of the ocean. Sailboats and fishing boats, the sun glittering off the water. Sometimes you could see whitecaps—it was probably rough out there, but in the distance everything looked perfectly still. I used to wonder where those sailboats were bound. I could imagine them plying the North Atlantic, headed east, headed south.

Now I'm lucky if I can get a glimpse of Commerce Street.

I lift the phone off its cradle. I set it down again. I look around.

O.K. Maybe I ought to get started here.

WHEN I ENTER the kitchen, Brenda is standing by the counter, smiling at the backs of her hands—I can't say how I arrive at these moments. There is silence, except from the verandah, where the bamboo wind chimes are clacking in the breeze. Other sounds, from the yard and beyond, percolate from that direction too: the twittering of birds, the distant fuss of a crow, sporadic fits of restlessness among the trees bordering the lawn. The late afternoon light gives the pale kitchen walls a look of ripeness as if, at long last, something is on the verge of happening here, something that may have been incubating for months. On the wall beside the fridge, the hands of the clock appear stuck at 5:47. Any of these details, I am willing to believe, may be significant.

Leaning against the cabinets, my wife loses interest in her hands and directs her smile at me. Her shirt is smudged with yellow and green paint, and she smells of turpentine. I almost can't look at her. Her beauty is just that devastating. Brenda, Goddess of the Late Afternoon Light. What I ought to do is sweep her into my arms. It would take hardly any effort at all. I could lift her like a bundle of swan feathers and transport her up the stairs to bed. The woman deserves no less.

"Did you remember to stop for bread?" she says.

It is actually a relief being brought back down to earth—particularly since, yes, I successfully remembered the bread. I flip the door to the breadbox and there it is open to her gaze, one pumpernickel, one baguette. It occurs to me I may have remembered other things too, though offhand I can't think what those might be. "I have a pretty good memory," I say.

Her expression wavers, as if she might want to challenge me on this.

"What?" I say.

"Having a good memory. That reminds me of something." She stares into the floor tile. "But I forget what."

"I've been there."

Brenda's stare slides over to the bread. She chews her lip. Then brightens. "Oh! The Legacy," she says. "It's due for an inspection."

"Hm!" I say.

"In fact, I think it's overdue."

"Son of a gun."

"Shoot, I meant to do that this morning. And tomorrow I'm helping Ted hang that show." She looks at me.

Ted I'll talk about later. My facial expression, as I imagine it, communicates something like a reflective pause. I'm supposed to be thinking it over. I'm supposed to be considering whether such an arrangement is possible, my taking care of the inspection.

But I see now this is lost on Brenda, whose attention has again zeroed in on her hands, where she may be discovering fresh paint smudges.

I open the fridge, select a bottle of water.

The truth is we sold the Legacy years ago.

It should be the most natural thing in the world for me to explore this discrepancy with my wife. But something in her manner seems to argue against it.

My reflective pause is frankly running on a bit long.

"I could do it," I say.

"You're a sweetheart."

It takes a moment to register, but now invading the yard outside is a repetitive metallic squeak. The gardener is walking by the verandah behind a wheelbarrow heaped with something that looks like red dirt. That's right. I neglected to mention we have a gardener. His name is Swenson. He more or less comes with the place.

As he passes, pushing his wheelbarrow, he throws a glance vaguely in our direction, but a bit over our heads, as though he might be appraising the tint of our roof shingles. But as is often the case with Swenson, I can't help feeling there is more to it than that. I detect in the gesture something along the lines of a taunt. I don't know what it is. When it comes to Swenson, I've made every effort to communicate respect for the work he does—his expertise, for example, in the business of growing things and later cutting things down. Still it seems the man harbors some stubborn resentment.

The late afternoon glow is fading. The ripeness of the kitchen walls, too, appears to have gone by. I twist the cap off the water bottle. The next step, I guess, would be to raise the bottle to my lips. But I don't. One minute has become another minute has become another minute. If anything is clear, it's that I'm not carrying Brenda up the stairs to bed. I don't exactly know how to say this, but sometimes there's a darkness around the edges of what can be seen. That alone is enough to make you hold back.

The thing is, too, I don't want to overdo it. When it comes to love, one can express only so much. Any more than that, it can give the wrong impression. I have a pervasive weakness for women anyway. Simple things can be the most affecting. Contemplation of the feminine collarbone, for example. I'm thinking of the other evening, that Romanian waitress, her blouse wide open at the neck, although perfunctorily—as far as she's concerned, it's just her uniform, and she's having a busy night. I'm supposed to be deliberating on the Bordeaux, but I've lost track of that responsibility somewhere in the territory between her throat and her breast. When we finally make eye contact, I've forgotten that I'm holding the menu. My pulse is racing.

Or long-legged Sonya entering my office, that delirious yearning of hers slightly blurring her presence. Who knows what it is she hungers for? Women—they're moving obliquely, it seems, and always a little further away. Sonya deposits a file on my desk. Or it could be something else. I can't take my eyes off her, yet by the time she is out the door, I understand that I haven't actually seen her. Once—just once—I'd like to ask her simply to stand still for me, so that I could at last get my fill of her.

Not that I would ever be unfaithful to my wife—I wouldn't even consider it. Really, despite my profound regard for the feminine form generally, I've never seriously been tempted by other women. Brenda has everything I need. Her incomparable, careless beauty. Her cool-burning, delicious, unaccountable apartness. She is continually a challenge and a delight. We've been together now for close to ten years, and I can say every moment with her is entirely new. Sure, at times it can be a little frightening.

Then, of course, there is the bedroom. Even during the dark years, we always had that. My God, lovemaking with Brenda!—in my prior life I couldn't have imagined the ecstasy. The deft attention to one another's pleasures. The daily sweet, lingering anticipation. To go into more detail I'm afraid would violate a sacred trust. I think it's enough to say that Brenda and I have rid ourselves of the inhibitions stifling so many marriages. Fairly often we use thick, soft ropes. After all, according to Brenda, the person bound hand and foot has no need of inhibition, has no need of a will, for that matter. I can feel all volition draining away, just talking about it. But already I may have said too much.

A Tangible Feeling

AT THE EDGE of the meadow we see the snake. The meadow looks familiar. It is the one he spotted earlier from his car window. Higher meadow, he called it, pressing his foot then more firmly on the gas pedal. In fact the ground lies some three-hundred feet above his accustomed route of travel—above the road, in other words, connecting his workplace with his home. Along the meadow's western boundary winds that other road—the one that appeared to stir darker imaginings in him, the one he claimed he had never seen before. Now and again it happens, and it's bound to come as a shock, this sudden manifestation of a thing that has been there all along.

The snake is moving the way a snake does, choosing its path slowly, insinuating itself among stalks of timothy, plantain, fireweed. Goldenrod, harebell, wool grass. Perfectly ordinary weeds. The air is still. With the snake's passing, the flowering tops and boles of the weeds quiver.

What is it about a snake that so inspires human ambivalence? We admire its disinterest and its silent grace at the same time we are nagged by suspicions of guile and stealth. There is all that lore to worry about: instantaneous death by venom, slow death by strangulation, the vulnerability of orifices. In the case of this particular animal, such fears might easily be magnified by the fact of its length—well over six feet. The presence of such an unlikely reptile in this largely suburban zone at the edge of forest inevitably raises questions, but they are not what interests us at the moment. We are watching the snake as it threads its way along the edge of the meadow, sloughing off speculation like old skin. It may be a matter of minutes. Or longer still. What is time to a snake? This one is obviously not in a hurry. And neither are we.

The snake appears to move deliberately. It wends this way and that way among the weeds and then pauses, wends and then pauses again. The effect is mesmerizing. Advancing somehow in its own track, the snake seems actually to *be* motion, rather than *in* motion. The reptile's scales are keeled, its skin colored according to a lopsided geometry. On a green background, darker lozenges repeat along its length. A bright stripe marks the spine. The snake, observed as it passes, is continually the same and continually different, recurring and flowing like a runnel of paint. We imagine that we hear it, but we don't.

Now, without warning, the snake spills forward. Now, without warning, it pauses. Its head turns, homing in our direction. Its tongue flicks out, testing.

I'M CONTEMPLATING reading a memo, something about strategic planning, when Stan wanders into my office. Our eyes connect, but he continues past my desk and stops in front of the window to inspect the view. Or what used to be the view. Now I assume he's seeing what I've had to look at for the past couple of weeks: essentially a field of gray, leaking faint impressions of the parking lot and whatever else is down there. If you look carefully during moments of brightening, you can make it all out—the strips of lawn and shrubbery and bark mulch, the walkways, the flags limp on their poles. And, across what I imagine to be the road, there's just a smudge of shadow where the UnitOne Building should be. All, I guess you could say, in readiness. For what? one might ask.

Stan leans into the window, craning left and right, as if he suspects something has been left out. Then he turns. He parks himself in his usual spot on the table. His eyes look red, as if he's been crying. He doesn't say anything. I don't say anything either, but I stop working.

Stan is probably my best friend at Argus, though it's a friendship requiring imagination. He doesn't communicate much. And when he does, it's almost never about work or sports or politics or any of those subjects friends usually bond over. He seems to be looking beyond all of that, at the next thing, the more essential thing, whatever that might be. The fact is it's hard to predict, at any given moment, what might come out of Stan's mouth. Maybe he's a little philosophical. His talk can get you thinking about things in ways you might not otherwise. But coming across Stan, say in the copy room, is not, in any conventional sense, a social encounter.

Still, it seems I can't let go of Stan. He's like nothing else in my life. He's like a little piece of it headed in the other direction. In the parking lot after a day at Argus we'll both be standing with our car doors open, not quite ready to surrender to the solace of those new interiors, but not able either to comprehend what it is we've just been through. We're tempted to think it's something, this devotion to rooms and corridors and screens so whitely lighted but only half-remembered. It may be we're even a little dazed. Eight, ten hours, often more—why wouldn't we be? Standing, staring through the yellow paint lines on the pavement, Stan will look as though he may at last have figured it out, as though he may be about to state a position. I'd certainly like to hear it. Leaning on the car door, he'll shake his head. "I don't know," he'll say, as though there's more to follow. But there isn't.

That's the way it is with Stan, as if he's taken up residence in the interstices of what the rest of us would call life. Associating with him feels actually dangerous. He's not a popular guy at Argus. To make matters worse, he's lost faith in the mission: expanding the data base, he's not sure he likes the idea. But I believe the company can't afford to get rid of him. He's one of the best crackers in the business. There is good reason to be afraid of him, afraid of what he could do if he left the company, especially on unfriendly terms. Vince, I get the feeling, is not exactly thrilled about my friendship with Stan. Silent people, around here, are regarded with suspicion.

But today Stan breaks the silence.

He says, "I think I may be allergic to rhododendrons."

It takes a while for these words to come into focus. Even then I'm slow to answer. "Why do you say that?" I try reading his face. I'm not convinced that allergy is what he wants to talk about.

Stan ignores my question. He seems even a little agitated. "It's basically an adversarial relationship with nature. I don't like it."

"I don't know," I say. "Rhododendrons aren't exactly nature."

He looks at me. "You may have a point."

Stan lives in Brandewoode too. There are maybe six or seven of us at Argus who do. Stan is the only one I care about. The others, if I see them—which I usually don't—I'll nod or wave, and that's that. There are fundamental forces operating here, the ones that draw certain people together and keep others apart. I've thought about this. The forces might as well be molecular, or subatomic. Which is to say, it does no good to talk about them. Like it or not, whenever Stan appears, I feel that gravitational tug. Too bad he and Brenda don't get along. I can never get a good word out of either one of them about the other.

Stan has had a privileged background: moneyed family, good schools, trips abroad. But he seems to have left all of that behind. I find these things out from other people. He never talks about any of it.

"All those red blossoms," Stan says. "Like mouths."

Which sets me to contemplating the devouring potential of rhododendrons. I'll grant there is a certain gorgeous creepiness about them.

Outside the window the fog is so thick, it's coming down as drizzle again, beading on the glass.

"Though you don't know, either," I say tentatively. "It may not be rhododendrons. It could easily be something else. Considering all the weeds out there."

"Weeds," he says, as though this were the last straw.

Now Vince pokes his head in through the doorway. His eyes fall immediately on Stan. He raises his eyebrows, withdraws.

Stan acts as though he didn't even see Vince. He says, "Weeds, Michael, are a thing of the past."

I don't quite have the nerve to answer this.

He says, "Cultivation is all the rage now. Everywhere you look, azaleas, lawn."

I'm shaking my head.

"All ducks in a row," he says. "That's the mantra these days."

"Oh, I don't know about that."

He raps a finger on the table for emphasis. "Except for the snakes. Christ, I'd almost forgotten about them."

I nod. But then I say, "What snakes?"

"Don't tell me you haven't noticed."

"What?"

"I see three or four a day now. Slithering out from under every rock and cranny. There was an article in the paper. Conditions this year are perfect."

I don't know whether to take him seriously. I say, "I haven't heard a thing about it."

"A banner year for snakes."

From outside now I hear the loud exhaust of a vehicle passing on the street below, which I imagine to be a motorcycle. Neither of us goes to the window. We can imagine whatever vehicle we want just as easily where we are. We don't need to be staring into that mist. Only after the sound has faded does Stan slide off the table and stand again, hands in his pockets, surveying what there is to be seen through the glass.

After a minute he says, as if to himself, "I wonder if nature even exists anymore."

"Sure it does." I say this emphatically.

"Where?"

I have to think for a moment. I'm recalling it even as I'm saying it. "Sometimes, standing out in the yard . . . I can feel it."

Stan turns to give me a measuring look. "Well, then. Good for you, Michael. Good for you." His voice sounds sincere. He turns back toward the window.

Just then the phone rings.

I **'M IN MY CAR,** headed north through the usual traffic on Route 17. I don't remember getting here. For these fifteen miles, I might as well have been asleep. This isn't the first time. I don't recall leaving my office, taking the elevator, or even entering my car. Anyway here I am, negotiating rush hour just like everyone else. I seem to fit right in.

Never mind that I've blanked out most of it, the drive home seems to drag on too long. Impatient for my exit sign, I'm beginning to imagine the road is unfamiliar. I feel a flutter of panic. Then at last the sign does appear. The anxiety passes. I don't know what's wrong. Maybe my mind is still stuck on the conversation with Stan—all that about snakes and weeds.

Eventually I pull into the driveway. Home at last. Stepping from the car onto the asphalt, however, I am not reassured. One ought to expect at least this of a front yard—it should provide comfort, a safe harbor. Mine, on this afternoon, does not. First there are the rhododendrons. I eye those pretty closely. They appear tranquil enough, in a menacing kind of way. As a matter of fact, all life in the familiar sprawl of lawn, azalea, boxwood, and forsythia seems blanketed under a peculiar hush. I ascend the steps to the flat sound of my own shoe soles scuffing against the stone, a sound somehow false, louder than it needs to be. The front door, I notice, is slightly ajar.

I don't know what I'm expecting. Moving through the house cautiously, I find Brenda in the kitchen. She's standing at the window, staring off toward the trees bordering the yard, apparently absorbed in her thoughts. There is a glass of wine in her hand. She seems a portrait of contentment.

She turns to me, and her eyes flare. "Whoa," she says, "you look annihilated."

I hang my jacket on the back of a chair.

"Want me to cook?" she says.

"That's O.K. It'll help me to wind down."

It is true, I generally do the cooking, what there is of it. It's not that she can't cook. She's quite good at it. But Brenda has a way of saving herself, and I admire her for that. There are better moments, I'm forced to admit, more suitable occasions, when I'm happy to watch her applying her talents.

We married, Brenda and I, straight out of college. We'd known each other a couple of years, after meeting through a computer dating service. The system they were using at the time calculated our Compatibility Quotient at 99.95, a value virtually unheard of. Getting matched up with my wife was how I was introduced to computers. Back then it felt a little scary, becoming a part of a data base, more or less giving yourself up to fate---the sort of thing that these days you simply take for granted.

Now Brenda moves away from the window to pour a second Cabernet.

"Here," she says, offering it to me. She presents it like a tribute, level with the V-neck of her aquamarine blouse, just above the slope of her breasts. Wine the color of garnet quivers in the glass. I feel a wave of weakness.

My hand reaches out, as if for the glass. She follows through, and my fingers close around it.

"Thanks," I hear myself say.

"Did you have a rough day?"

I shrug the question off. "No worse than usual. I don't know what's the matter with me."

"Maybe you're coming down with something."

I'm in and out of the fridge now, opening and closing cabinet doors, putting the dinner together. At the edge of my vision I can feel her watching.

Now she moves closer, as if to nuzzle against me. But she stops short of contact.

She says, "Have you been smoking?"

I look at her. "No, of course not."

"You smell like cigarettes."

"Oh. Right. It's that NewBank executive. Marjorie Lundstrom."

"I thought they didn't allow that anymore, smoking in the workplace."

"Yeah, well, Marjorie's one of the holdouts."

After a pause, Brenda's voice turns sly. "So, this Marjorie . . . this is a woman you spend a lot of time with?"

"Actually, I've never met her. I just talk to her over the phone. Or I should say, she talks to me. And I pretend to listen."

The salad is ready. I can hear the water for the pasta coming to a boil.

Brenda's voice is measured. "You're telling me you soaked up this woman's cigarette smoke over the telephone lines."

Leaning, both hands on the counter, I hear the microwave beep, indicating the clams have thawed. I'm feeling unaccountably exhausted. I can barely think, much less bring myself to respond. "That's the way it seems," I say. I reach, flip open the microwave door.

Carrying the tray with the salad, I notice Brenda standing a little apart, her wine glass poised in the air somewhere above her right shoulder. She's watching me. Only her eyes move.

We're midway through eating dinner over the click clack of our knives and forks when Brenda says, "Oh, something got into the trash last night."

I look up from my plate.

She says, "Whatever it was lifted one of those huge galvanized cans clear out of the bin and set it on the driveway."

"Hm!" I tear a roll in half. "It's a wonder we didn't hear it."

"Then it took the cover off, set that on the ground, and removed the top two bags to get at the bottom bag."

"I'll be damned."

"Apparently it was after the chicken bones."

I'm shaking my head. I don't like the sound of this.

"But that isn't all," she says. "Instead of ripping through the last bag, the way you'd expect, to get at the bones, it undid the ties." She nods for emphasis, looking me straight in the eye. "Whatever it was undid the ties."

"It had to have been a person."

"That's what I thought. That's exactly what I thought." She spears a clam with her fork. "But what sort of person pokes through someone else's garbage to get at their rotten chicken bones?"

I turn to the diningroom window, which offers a view out across the lawn to the border of the woods beyond. The light is uneasy, mingled with shadow, anticipating evening. "Right," I say. I can't think of anything else to say.

I'M THINKING of the way Brenda enters a room, as though descending from her own dreams. She could be holding, let's say, a magazine—even though there are no magazines in this house and, as far as I know, never have been. But she's holding one (it occurs to me only afterward). Or let's say that she is carrying a cup of tea, steaming hot, which she has come by somehow. And this is exactly a part of what I mean. I've never actually seen my wife make a cup of tea, odd as that may sound. No matter, she'll suddenly appear with one, looking splendid, as Brenda always does. Nor has she ever worn reading glasses, yet there she'll be, a pair in her hand. Where does she come up with these things?—sweeping carelessly into the scene as if bearing gifts out of heaven.

Yesterday afternoon, returning from work, I found her out on the chaise longue, reading. I stood, smiling down at her through the window from the relative darkness of the den. She certainly couldn't see me, though I could observe her plainly, barely five feet away. I reached to tap lightly on the glass, a playful greeting. Then I stopped myself.

There was something in the moment—an almost forbidden fullness. I wasn't about to spoil it. No, I stood there, admiring her fine legs. She was half-lying, half-sitting, her one leg extended, the other nonchalantly flexed, a pose drawing attention to the trim contour of her thigh where it finally rounded to buttock before disappearing beneath the hem of her shorts. I watched as her foot stirred against the chaise cushion. Something seemed to pass through me then. I steadied myself with two fingers against the glass. I took in a long, delirious breath. I knew well the fragrance of her skin. The glass was hardly more than a theoretical barrier. Her bare midriff rose and fell, and I thought I could actually hear her breathing until I realized it was my own.

It was then for the first time that I felt just a touch of regret. Not that I thought I was doing anything wrong. A man had to be free, after all, to enjoy the sight of his own wife. But it was clear, too, that there were limits, though I couldn't be sure what those were. In any case, sooner or later, Brenda would rise from her chaise, whisk herself inside, and that would be the end of it. For the moment, however, my eyes were having their way with her.

Sweet Brenda, for her part, was wholly immersed in her reading, her stare fixed on the pages of her book. I was so close I could make out the page number and chapter heading. I knew the book, a recent critique of contemporary art—"*PAINTING, SCULPTURE, MIXED MEDIA, AND BEYOND,*" the subtitle read. As a matter of fact, the day before, I'd picked it up and browsed ahead of her bookmark. Absolutely. I take an active interest in my wife's intellectual life. So, as she lay there transitioning from page 237 to page 238, utterly available to my eyes, I had a pretty good idea where her mind was too. Coming to terms with demonstration art and the aesthetic flux of global culture, I estimated. Should art stand in opposition to materiality or embrace it? Is the economy the new and final art form? These were the sort of questions awash in my wife's consciousness as she lay there, the object of my lust.

I watched as she flipped back to page 237, the shadow of a wrinkle writing itself across her brow. She looked out meditatively toward the woods bordering the yard, and the afternoon seemed to advance one notch closer to evening.

It was then it registered. I thought I'd just heard someone upstairs open a window.

I 'VE NEVER HAD much use for dreams. According to some people, dreams are like messengers, freshly arrived from our subconscious—with advice. Certainly the dream world has its place. But we'd all be a lot better off, I think, if it stayed there, tucked away behind our tightly closed eyelids. Pieces of it shouldn't be wriggling free, contaminating our actual lives. It's a recipe for confusion.

Just as an example, I remember once years ago having a powerful urge to hear a certain record album I owned. This actually happened. I spent well over an hour searching through my record collection, more and more frantically looking for it. Somehow it seemed to have disappeared. It didn't help that I couldn't recall the title or the name of the band. But I had a clear enough memory of the music and the effect it had had on me. My rummaging continued on and off for days, with me once again pulling each album—one at a time—out of the stacks and staring at it, probing under furniture and behind doors, and otherwise ransacking my apartment. I was acting, and feeling, like some sort of deprived creature. I thought at some point maybe I'd loaned the album to someone who hadn't bothered to return it. Then I imagined it had been stolen.

Eventually I came to my senses and realized that I'd never actually owned such an album to begin with, that in fact no such album existed, and that, incredible as it seemed, I'd only dreamt that it had. And still—still!—I was burning to listen to it. I felt actually cheated. To this day, there is a place reserved among my memorable experiences for the pleasure that album gave me—a purely dreamed-up pleasure over a music that never was.

Ridiculous.

Ever since that episode, I've been wary of experiences that come to me during sleep. In fact, now more than ever. One dream in particular recently has been nagging away at me. The basic scenario is this: I'm waiting for an elevator. This is in the corridor at Argus, seventh floor, or some place more or less like that. I've hit the down button, and I'm standing, waiting. I don't wait long. The bell rings and the door opens, and suddenly I'm looking at an elevator full of people, and all of them have the same face.

They're all staring out at me. Of course, I'm about the only thing they have to look at. But every single one of them has the same face—men, women, short, tall, in suits, dresses. Merely the idea of it I guess could be hilarious, but in my dream I'm not laughing. And afterward when I wake up, which is usually right after this dream, I'm not laughing either. There is nothing funny about it. The opposite, in fact. The moment that elevator door rolls open, I am immobilized with fear.

Now, considering the fact that I've dreamed this scene maybe half a dozen times, you might expect I'd be able to describe the face peering back at me from that crowd of bodies. The truth is I find it next to impossible. There seems, I do recall, something missing about the eyes. And the skin appears overall sickly, like the color of an egg carton. The rest of it I can't remember. Maybe there's a little too much red about the mouth. I've heard it said that the face is the mirror of the soul. I would not want to be the soul gazing into that particular mirror.

Sure, it's only a dream. And, no, I haven't run across any of those faces lurking in the shadows or riding elevators, for that matter. But I have to say, with certain people at Argus, I have had cause to look twice. Dave in Financial Services, and Gil over in Marketing. Even Carol up in Human Resources. Nothing comes of it. There's just a momentary glimmer of resemblance, but it's enough to throw me off. I lose track of the conversation. With Gil the other day (wearing that stupid broad-brimmed hat of his), I blanked out so thoroughly, the poor guy walked off and left me standing in the parking lot. If this keeps up, how long before word gets around? Michael Benson, popcorn head.

Saturday morning I'm upstairs in my study, reading poetry, of all things. Anthology, it says on the jacket—I don't know how many poems there are in here. It's been a good while since I've tackled anything remotely like this, but I'm pretty well determined to go ahead with it. So far, it's been one riddle after another, though every once in awhile, a glint of something. Like the lines, describing a robin,
> And he unrolled his feathers
> And rowed him softer home—
> Than Oars divide the ocean,
> Too silver for a seam—

Nice, I thought, when I came to that. But a lot of it I'm just fidgeting my way through. There is, as you might expect, a story behind this.

It happened the other evening. I inadvertently got a glimpse of one of Brenda's recent creations, one of her "works in progress," as she calls them. Understand, my wife is a bit sensitive about her art. She never, under any circumstances, shows her paintings until they're finished. Often even then I don't see them. Well, I saw this one. For all I could tell, it *was* finished—an honest accident, but it went over badly with Brenda. So did my reaction, which might more or less accurately be described as openmouthed bewilderment.

Brenda wasted no time turning the painting to the wall. "Don't say a word," she said. "I don't want to hear it." That was bad enough on the surface of it, but what bothered me more was the *way* she'd said it, as if she were dealing with some vulgarian. I tried to make light of it, but the remark stung. Probably—I realized later—because she actually had a point.

Over the years I haven't had a lot of time for what you call art. I've been too busy pretending to earn a living, and otherwise trying to maintain whatever equilibrium is possible in times like these. The few encounters I've had with painting, sculpture, poetry, and so on have generally left me feeling stupid—an experience I haven't been eager to repeat. But since that incident the other evening, I've had occasion to reconsider. In a matter so dear to my wife, it seems to me, it wouldn't hurt to educate myself. Better late than never. So here I am in my study on a precious Saturday morning, launching my attention into the tricky waters of poetry.

Now, hearing voices, I glance up from the page to gaze out my window. It takes me a minute to spot Brenda over at the edge of the yard, where a narrow border of weeds separates the lawn from the woods. She is standing—my lovely wife—in a most revealing pair of shorts, hands on her hips, looking down into the grass. And talking. Apparently, it is only her voice I hear.

Brenda, Brenda, Brenda. Sweet distraction of my life, how is your husband supposed to attend to poetry? Brenda of course does not answer this question, though she is saying *something*. Who on earth is she talking to? Standing that way, her attention directed down, she looks for all the world to be carrying on a conversation with the lawn. What next?

Later in the kitchen Brenda informs me that last night our trash was raided again. An almost identical modus operandi. Only this time, instead of chicken bones, the thing was after crab legs.

I have been making iced tea, but at this news my gaze wanders out toward the lawn. "Weird," I say. It annoys me, this niggling breach of security. Probably more than it should. Something has moved in from God knows where and, in its own miniscule way, has begun eating away at our lives. Or that's the way it seems.

I go back to making iced tea. And then it occurs to me: I ask Brenda about her little conversation earlier out on the lawn.

"What?" she says

I feel a little foolish repeating the question.

"Oh, that," she says, laughing. "There was a snake at the edge of the lawn."

I have the pitcher lodged under the ice machine, ice cubes cascading, clattering into it. I think I didn't hear her right. "A what?"

"A snake. You should have seen it. The thing must have been seven feet long."

"Not in New England, Brenda. We don't have snakes that big here."

"Well, you should have seen this one."

I'm slicing lemon, eight little crescents. I grin, but I'm not really amused. "So you were . . . talking to the snake?"

Brenda is rummaging in one of the utensil drawers. "Sure, I like snakes."

I lift the lid on the tea pot. The brew is dark and gives off the right odor.

I ask, "What did you say to it?"

"What?"

"What did you have to say to a snake?"

"I don't know. What difference does it make?"

I spoon a little sugar onto the ice, watch as it sifts its way down, then pour the tea. "You have a conversation with a snake and you can't remember what was said?"

"For God's sake, Michael. O.K. I said 'Whoa, hello there, Mr. Snake. You're a big fellow. What can I do for you?'" She looks at me. "There, satisfied?"

I pour a couple of glasses full. I hand her one. I'm not going to say any more. Still, something about it bothers me.

A little later, while Brenda is in the shower, I go out by the edge of the lawn. I bring a golf club, a five iron, from the garage, just in case. But I can't see any snake.

The weeds are thick in that border along the edge of the woods. What look like brambles are mixed among the grasses. As I'm standing, everything around me is very still. There is a certain combination of sounds and smells. It occurs to me, the summer is nearly over. It seems as though it has hardly begun.

I think I'll mention the weeds to Swenson.

Mingled with Shadow

IT IS PERHAPS a little after sunset, though the term seems theoretical, given the thick overcast. Windows the length of Forest Avenue are already lighting up, the houses glowing from within, as if with awakening fires. Here outside, nothing moves. Every twig and blade of grass suffers the gray drizzle while the air steadily darkens.

But what is that?—there, just across from Michael's driveway, that lone figure standing on the curb between the light pole and the wall of hedges. Whether he is doing anything else, other than standing, is difficult to see. The streetlight overhead has not yet switched on. Perhaps in some other neighborhood someone like this might be assumed to be waiting for a cab or contemplating crossing the street. But not here, not on Forest Avenue, where cabs rarely deliver and pick up fares, and then only at front doors, and where no one ever crosses the street.

In this uncertain light, we can't see the face, but we're satisfied that the form is masculine, considering the shoulders, the shoe size, what looks like a dark suit and tie, and some sort of broad-brimmed hat. Whoever he is, we've never encountered him before. Even without a clear view of him, we're somehow convinced of this.

At last the overhead streetlight flickers on, casting a halo of drizzle around the lamp itself and to some extent brightening the scene. But the face of this stranger (who seems hardly there to begin with) remains stubbornly in shadow beneath the brim of that hat, so intent is he, apparently, on something in his hand, something he is manipulating. Perhaps a cell phone. Now, in the house behind him, a light pops on in an upstairs window. And then another. But these don't illuminate him either. Each new light in the scene, in fact, serves merely to accentuate the dark.

Now, however, the stranger turns. Light spills across one side of the face, and we take a quick breath, for it is nothing like the kind of face we were expecting. What can be said of it?—other than that, yes, it is where a face ought to be. Still we don't know what it is we're seeing, the features have so thoroughly warped from what we would recognize as human. There are what might be eyes, small and black, empty as holes. The skin (if that's what it is) has the color, even the crinkly texture, of old paper. Beyond that, it is difficult even to look at this face: the tumid lips, the caved-in cheeks. Perhaps, too, we could be persuaded, there is something like an expression—the opposite of surprise.

Now movement. By the time we realize, it has already happened. Gradually, the figure has been absorbed by the hedges, and we are left wondering what it is we've seen, or whether we've seen anything at all.

THERE IS SONYA'S sudden voice in the outer office. I recognize instantly where I am. But there is also that split-second remembrance—of where would be difficult to say. A feeling like fire and ice, along with some dreadful urgency. Of course that makes no sense. I'm not sure even how to talk about these things. I know this much: it's like a particular flavor of the mind, beckoning. But I wouldn't be able to name it or find my way back there if my life depended on it.

Anyway there is Sonya's voice.

And then Vince Marconi is in the door, and with him Wendell Carlson, Eastern Division Vice President, along with some guy I'm sure I've never seen before. Gray suit, big ears, prominent Adam's apple. Somebody—Wendell says, smiling—he wants me to meet. Vince is smiling too. I pay attention. Normally you couldn't buy a smile from Vince.

Lying open beside my keyboard, I quickly realize, is a small volume of poetry.

"Michael," Wendell says, "this is Jack Folsom. Coordinator of Strategic Planning."

Jack reaches.

I don't hesitate. I rise to take his hand. He has a bit of a limp grip, Jack. Strategic Planning—somehow it rings a bell.

"Good to meet you," I say. I set a file folder on top of the poetry.

Jack is nodding, looking past me, toward the window. He says, "Nice view you have here."

I glance at the framed panorama of fog. I don't say anything. There is something about Jack's eyes.

Vince quietly shuts the door to the outer office.

Wendell half-sits, resting his butt on the corner of my desk—here at Argus, an unmistakable gesture of intimacy.

I sit, and I invite them to sit too. There are enough chairs. But no one makes a move.

Wendell engages Vince in a little playful small talk, really not worth repeating. I listen, my expression—as I imagine it—one of ready congeniality.

They spar for a minute. Then the conversation turns, as I suspected it would, to Jack.

"You got the memo," Wendell says.

I can't deny it. So I nod. All the time I'm maintaining eye contact.

But then maybe there *is* something at the window—a quick movement or a brightening. I turn, and it may be that I see something, but I'm not sure. When I look back, Wendell, Vince, and Jack are all staring at the window. But no one says anything.

Wendell's voice turns warm, fatherly. We're all going to be seeing quite a bit more of Jack, he explains. Over the next several months, Strategic Planning will be canvassing, working its way through the various departments, soliciting input. "Phase One," Wendell says.

"Assessment," Vince adds.

Wendell aims a finger at me as if it were the barrel of a gun. "S.W.O.T." he says.

I nod, putting some emphasis into it, as though this is the piece of the puzzle I've been waiting for.

Wendell elaborates, "Strengths, Weaknesses, Opportunities, Threats. Broken down, department by department."

Vince is nodding gravely. In case his approval was in doubt.

"You'll have your turn of course." Wendell's expression is glowing so warmly, I'm almost looking forward to it. Having my turn.

"Jack's a regular bulldog," Vince says with a wink. "You won't get away from him."

"He'll be talking to everyone," Wendell says.

At the moment, I can't help noticing, Jack isn't talking to anybody. Instead, he seems to be conducting a silent inventory of the furniture in my office.

Wendell says, "We're expecting the Design Phase'll be in place sometime next April. Then Implementation by, say, September. At the latest."

There is more of this talk. Through most of it, I'm struggling not to lose the thread. I'm wishing I had read the memo.

Eventually they leave.

Alone in my office, I feel a sensation, a tightening, dead-center in my chest.

I'm in the back yard, carrying out the trash, an undertaking a little more complicated now than it used to be. I've bought a chain and a lock to secure the lids onto the cans. I hang the key on a nail I drove into the clapboards under a little sign that reads, "TRASH CAN KEY, HELP YOURSELF." This is what comes of being a security specialist. I'm figuring, if whatever it is after our trash uses the key, that proves it's a person. Whereas, an animal——say a raccoon—won't be able to read the sign. Maybe it will rattle the chains a bit, but then move on to the neighbors'. My own little strategic plan.

I told Brenda about it. She looked at me, narrowing her eyes almost to a squint. I thought she was going to say something, but she didn't.

Anyway, I'm clipping the lock back onto the chain when I notice Swenson over by the edge of the lawn. Oddly enough, he appears to be raking leaves. It seems a little early in the year, if you ask me. On the other hand, if anyone knows trees, it's Swenson. I'm not about to second-guess the man on matters arboreal.

The fact is Swenson is not exactly a gardener—I don't even know why I said that. Certainly, he takes care of a few gardens among the properties. But most of the common land in Brandewoode is wooded: those beauty strips I mentioned. So really he's more like a forester, a term you hardly hear these days. The guy is maybe forty, about my age. According to Brenda, he's been to college. But whether he studied forestry or genetic engineering, or whether indeed he studied at all I couldn't say.

But here he is in our back yard, and here I am. I've finished putting out the trash, and I've about exhausted the time I could reasonably spend lingering around the cans.

It's not that I decide to talk to Swenson. It's more that I find myself, hands in pockets, ambling in his direction. I'm a good fifty feet from him, but already something in the set of his jaw tells me he has noticed. So now I'll have to follow through. Either that or look like a fool.

I'm not sure what I'm going to say. Swenson is not an especially friendly guy. He never speaks unless spoken to. When he greets you at all, it's with a simple nod. You might say there's a trace of an attitude about him, vaguely militant working class. Not that I have any quarrel with the working class, but with him it seems to have become a kind of creed.

"Hello, Swenson," I say.

His head bobs. He doesn't stop raking.

I inspect the ground around his rake, and, sure enough, the lawn there is spotted with yellowed leaves from the ginkgo. The leaves remaining on the tree are turning yellow also, brightening the gloom of the fog overhead, which seems now as though it might be thinning. For the moment it has stopped drizzling. I say, "Not a lot left of summer, I guess."

He chuckles.

"It shouldn't be long now," I say.

"No." He continues raking, corralling those odd yellow leaves with quick, vigorous strokes. "Not very long," he says. "Not very long at all." His voice is resigned, almost wistful. I wonder whether we're talking about the same thing.

"Well . . . ." I direct my eyes toward the nearby woods. "Who can say?"

Swenson switches hands on the rake, so he winds up facing slightly away from me. It's as if we've both taken an interest in those woods.

I come to the point. "Say, Swenson, you haven't seen any large snakes around here lately, have you?"

He abruptly stops raking and gives me a suspicious look.

"Yeah, it's weird, a couple of days ago," I say, "apparently we had a pretty big one. Right over there. In those weeds."

He glares at the weeds where I'm pointing. "Oh." He goes back to raking, a little less vigorously now.

The rake, in Swenson's hands, looks like a toy. Across the front and back of his Forestry-issue green t-shirt, the word PARKS is emblazoned in gold lettering. The shirt is stretched tight over the muscles of his back and arms. He has big arms, Swenson.

I say, "Yeah, my wife was the one who saw it."

"The snake."

"She said it must have been seven feet long."

Swenson chuckles. "Paid you a visit, did he?"

"Yeah. So I was wondering . . . ."

"Yah, we got snakes. They say this is a year for 'em."

"As big as that, though?" I hold out my arms wide.

But he doesn't look. "Brandewoode, hell yah, we got snakes. Some big ones, and some little ones, and some in-between ones. You don't have nothing to fear from them. They ain't poisonous, our snakes." He's grinning now. "And they ain't constrictors."

"No, I know, I'm not afraid of them. I'm not afraid of snakes. It's just . . . ." My eyes cast about. I spot the bird feeder by the kitchen window. "I thought they might be after the birds."

"Well, yah, they might. It's true. They might."

Whatever brightening there was earlier in the sky seems to have reversed itself. The air hangs thick and damp, as if some influence from the woods has worked its way in over the yard.

"Anyway, Swenson, I was wondering if there might be something you could do about those weeds."

He stops raking. "What, that little strip of meadow there?"

"Right."

"That's a buffer," he says. "You want to cut that?" The question feels like a challenge.

We're both standing, surveying the meadow, as he calls it. It can't be more than four feet wide. I'm nodding. "Well it might not hurt to trim it down a little. What do you think?"

I'm looking at the size of his arms. I'm thinking maybe I could afford to work out a little.

Swenson is standing there, evaluating the strip of weeds. "Meadow," he says. He shakes his head.

T**HIS EVENING**, entering Brandewoode, I drive extra, extra slow. Ignoring my usual turnoff for some reason, I choose the less direct route, past the playground and the duck pond, to get onto Forest Avenue. I drive like a stalker. My foot isn't even on the gas pedal—that's how slow I'm going. Daylight is steadily draining away. I look carefully at everything: the shapes of trees, numbers on mailboxes, details I usually take for granted. At the intersection of Linden, a car turns in behind me and follows close. Immediately I pull over to the curb and let it pass.

Even though I'm coming at it from a different angle, what I see is what I always see here: the broad lawns under stately trees, glimpses of brick and clapboard and stone and window, suggesting homes behind these hedges. All of it flawless, or so it would seem. But in the failing light, I wonder.

I stop the car. I allow my eyes to take in everything, nothing.

I feel certain that something is missing. I'm not sure what I mean by that. Is it something that used to be here but is gone, or that never was here and I'm only now aware of? A kind of pressure builds behind my throat, as if, the next moment, I might cry.

It's been over a week since anyone has fiddled with our trash. So, yes, I'm convinced now it was a person. The sign must have put a scare into him, must have made him wonder, what next? His escapades might be video-recorded. Or worse. No, it appears that, whoever he is, he has moved on. There's no shortage of trash cans in the neighborhood.

Meanwhile I've been reading a lot more poetry. One poet after another after another. Now and then, a couple of lines will catch me off-guard and twist the world around in a new direction. Though often, I have to confess, my mind still wanders. I keep on reading, regardless, my eyes reckless over the pages. I like the feel of it that way, the words knocking around inside my head. If Brenda knew, she'd probably have a fit.

As a matter of fact, I hear my wife now in her studio across the hall—stretching canvases, it sounds like. I wouldn't mind having a peek at her, frankly. For close to an hour, I've been here in my study, faithfully reading some French poet—I can't pronounce his name. Though I have my eye on a particular Russian. I'm certainly not lacking for choices here. My desk is stacked to the ceiling with them. I reach to pick one up, pause to consider the title: *Leaves of Grass*. It's awfully hefty for a book of poetry, and my arms and wrists feel like rubber from doing pushups awhile ago. My life, it seems, is being taken over by exercise. If it isn't one muscle, it's another.

And now, in the midst of this (the book straining my grip to the breaking point) comes something else, like the nagging realization that I've forgotten something. But no, not that. Rather, I'm being watched! It seems odd that I know this, and odd also that I know from which direction. I look up from the book and out through the window to the lawn. There, by the edge of the woods, someone is standing—a woman, dressed from head to toe in gray. She could pass for a tree trunk if it weren't for those eyes, burning across that distance, staring straight at me. Or, the way it feels, *into* me.

She scares the blazes out of me. I jump, the *Leaves of Grass* slips from my grip, and then, as I reach for it, so does the French poetry along with my mug full of pencils. All of it crashes to the floor.

After a pause, I hear Brenda call. "Hey, what's going on? Michael! Are you O.K.?"

By the time I get to the window for a look, there's not a sign of that woman out there—not a trace. She's vanished. I'm there at the sash, craning my neck one way and then the other, when I hear Brenda's voice now behind me.

"Hey, are you all right?" she says. "Why didn't you answer?"

Turning around, I bump my head on the sash. And there, sure enough, is Brenda. She is standing—where I've never seen her before—at the door to my study.

"Sorry," I say, "I was . . . trying to get a better look."

"Look at what? What in the world was that noise?"

"Oh, I . . . dropped some stuff."

"What happened?"

"There was a . . . ." I glance back out at the lawn. Of course I'm ready to tell her, ready to blurt it out. I'm burning, really, to share it with someone, such a weird experience. My heart is pumping like mad. But, I don't know what it is, something stops me. I am mystified to hear myself say, "There was a raven."

"A what?"

I hold my hands out, maybe three feet apart. "Jesus, Brenda, the thing flew right up to the window. I thought it was headed, God, right in here."

Her mouth open, she stares at the window. Then her gaze shifts to the floor, then to my desk. She says, "Michael, what are you doing with all these books?"

Stan and I are in my office. He's leaning forward in my chair, working at my machine, and I'm sitting behind him, watching. We're teaming on a case, a break-in at ZACTRON, a potential customer. They've been relying on software provided by Cerberus, one of our competitors. I hammered away at the thing this morning for a couple of hours and couldn't find a seam big enough for a knife blade. The cracker, whoever he was, dipped into the company's payroll file, ate seven employees (as Stan put it, "just to show that he could"), and then evaporated.

We're both staring at the screen, Stan's fingers flying over the keyboard. He's been here about twenty minutes. I just got back from coffee.

Stan stops and strokes his chin as if he had a beard, which he doesn't. "A work of art," he says.

Then a minute later he says, "This guy is nuts."

"Rootkit?" I ask.

Stan shakes his head. "I think original. There's a level of subtlety here."

"You're sure it's an intrusion?"

"Yeah."

"Not a false positive?"

He looks at me. "Give me a little credit."

This is the way it works with us. The only way I get a peek at what Stan's thinking is to keep lobbing these softballs at him. I say, "It's not just a bug?"

"Oh, it's malicious all right. Put the first letters of the seven employees' last names together, it spells "Nice day.""

"Oh."

For awhile Stan doesn't say anything, his fingers clicking the keys.

I get up and wander over to the window. I stand right at the center of it, hands in my pockets, staring out as though I can actually see something. It has been three, four weeks—possibly longer—since I last looked out at that distant ocean. I guess I have to assume it's still there. Now there's nothing to see but this thick, interminable gray. Maybe over the weekend we could take a trip, Brenda and I. I'm beginning to feel a little claustrophobic.

The click of the keys stops.

I turn, and Stan is just sitting there. He seems distracted, listening for something over his shoulder. Then the other shoulder. He's sniffing the air. He looks at me.

"What?" I say.

He raises his arms, one at a time. He gets up and he comes for me, his nose homing in on my shirt.

"What are you doing?"

Stan is glancing around the room. "Have you noticed an odor lately?"

"Where?"

"I don't know. I smell it more sometimes than other times."

"Like where?"

"I don't know, everywhere. Basically I smell it everywhere. It's making me nervous. It starts in the morning on the way to work. And I smell it here, now."

"In my office?"

"And earlier too. All through this building. Through the whole building. I thought at first it might be the carpeting."

"What about at home?"

He considers this. "No, not there. Not yet." His eyes rove the room.

"What kind of odor?"

"I'm not sure." He opens one of my desk drawers and peers into it.

I'm a little shocked by this.

"Like an animal," he says. "A large animal."

"What, you mean like a bear?"

He opens another drawer, closes it. "I don't know. Whatever it is, it's pretty awful."

"Maybe it has something to do with your car. Maybe you hit a skunk." I watch him open another drawer. "What, you're ransacking my desk now?"

"Nah, nothing like skunk." Stan shuts the drawer. He moves over to the table, fidgeting.

I don't know what to say. My nose isn't much use to me. People are always noticing odors before I do. I'm inhaling long attentive breaths, sorting through the possibilities. It smells to me like my office, nothing more.

All of a sudden Stan turns from the window. His eyes fall on the computer screen. "Wait a minute," he says.

BACK AND FORTH—home to office, office to home. Of course that's what a good part of life boils down to. Then there are the moments when something jolts you out of the routine and draws your attention in a different direction, one you may have neglected. It's one thing to have your trash stolen. It's quite another when some woman—a complete stranger!—stands out on your lawn like a monument, staring into your window. And where the devil could she have come from, if not out of the woods?

So, yes, the woods. I've been conducting a little research. One thing I've learned is this: a long, long time ago, apparently, a terrific fire exploded out of this forest. A blaze of titanic proportions. The incident is how Brandewoode got its name. The flames destroyed all the homes in the area and most of the nearby town. However—this is according to Swenson—though the fire started in the forest, only certain portions of it burned. A grain of salt may apply here. Swenson can let himself get carried away with his sylvan lore. The forest, he maintains, has ways of protecting itself.

Well, that is neither here nor there. I'm more interested in protecting our privacy. So I've been keeping an eye on these woods, and I've been noticing things—the simple fact, for example, that there are gaps among the trees. Beauty strip or no beauty strip, I had always thought of forest as dense. "Impenetrable" is the word people use. But no, there's space to move around in there. With nothing more than an ordinary pair of binoculars from my study window, I can see it pretty plainly. I believe it would be possible, theoretically at least, to walk out our back door and into the woods in more or less a straight line and, if you chose the right direction, eventually come out in the back yard of one of our neighbors.

Of course, nobody ever does that—I don't know anyone who has. But, my point is, someone could.

And then I got to thinking, what if someone did and chose the *wrong* direction? What then? Which raises the question, what is the purpose of all those woods back there? That might be stating the case too strongly. I'm in no way denying the aesthetic value, or what some might call the spiritual dimension, of trees. Those years in the city taught me that much. I've enjoyed—as much as anyone could—the moments here on our screen porch, basking in the profound shadow and serenity of this apparent forest wall. All I'm saying is it might make sense to trim the woods back a little.

Though Swenson, I imagine, may be hard to persuade.

Adjusting my posture in the chair, I look over my shoulder. The house is awfully quiet tonight. Last I was aware of Brenda, she was downstairs somewhere, but for the past half-hour I haven't heard so much as a floorboard squeak. I'm here at my desk, a volume of Russian poetry in my lap, though I seem to have stopped reading some time ago. Instead I've been appreciating the night outside my window, the play of light against the leaves of the oaks. A breeze is moving the branches in the porch light. The leaves are translucent as green glass, but they cast long shadows into the drizzle and onto the lawn and the trunks of the trees.

The shadows flicker and squirm as if alive. I don't know how to say this exactly. It's not the sort of thing I'm used to seeing. There's something vaguely hungry about these shadows. They dart out from the points of the leaves unexpectedly, like cracks exploiting the weakness of evening. I can't take my eyes away.

I wonder what, if he were here, this Russian poet might have to say about these shadows. None of what I just said, probably.

Now I hear, remotely communicated through the walls and floor of the house, the little click of the porch light switch, and at the same time, all at once, my view of the oaks goes black. There isn't a thing to be seen through the window, only the dull glint of my desk lamp reflected in the upper sash. I stay perfectly still, listening, but I don't hear anything else.

I rise from my desk, stick my head out into the hall. Nothing.

Extra carefully, I descend the stairs. I don't know what I'm expecting. For some reason, at the entrance to the diningroom I pause. All those chairs set up around the diningroom table—there's something creepy about it. Except for the nightlights in the hall and in the kitchen, there are no lights on anywhere downstairs. Still, with the white walls, I can see just about everything. I'm standing, listening, but there isn't a sound. Not yet.

Then, from a location I can only imagine, somewhere out there in the night fog, something howls. Long and distant and mournful. Fifteen, twenty seconds later, it howls again, the sound this time, it seems, entering through a different window. Maybe, whatever it is, it's on the move. Or maybe there are two of them, out there in the pitch darkness.

But what else then? I'm sure there is something else.

"Brenda?" I say. My voice has never sounded more strange.

There's no answer. I don't like it. I'm convinced, on the other side of this silence, someone is there, listening.

What am I supposed to do? The moment has a weird, unconnected feel to it, as if I've been thrust out so far ahead of myself, I can't catch up. It's like being someone else, someone without a name, someone without even a face. That's the way it feels. And, I'm embarrassed to say, my first inclination is to grab something—something I can use as a weapon. I make a move toward the umbrella stand by the front door, but then stop myself.

"Brenda?" I repeat.

Still no answer.

In the kitchen again I pause. Then I flip on the porch light. It's like a challenge. Whoever turned the light off, maybe this will flush them out. Of course, it has to have been Brenda. Outside, through the screen, I can hear the wind increasing in the trees. But there is no seeing the shadows of those oak leaves from here.

The wall clock says close to ten. I stand waiting another two or three minutes, then head back upstairs to the bathroom to brush my teeth, leaving the porch light on. It's still on when I undress and sit on the bed. I can see the shadows, but the angle is wrong. It's not the same.

When I turn off the lamp by the bed, the glow from the porch light is enough to illuminate the room. I'm not lying in bed five minutes before I hear the switch again down there, and it all goes dark. Then Brenda is coming up the stairs.

In the bedroom she's so quiet I can hear her breathing.

As she slides into bed, I say, "Where were you?"

"Oh, reading," she says.

"Hm!" I say.

She doesn't say anything more.

For awhile I lie there, awake. I hear Brenda fall asleep before I do.

Saturday morning I'm loading the dishwasher. The doorbell rings, and I answer it. It's Ted. I tell him Brenda's in her studio. At least I think that's where she is. I ask him if he'd like a coffee. He thanks me, graciously enough, but says he drinks only maté now. "Aha," I say. I don't know maté from chicken soup. Ted's another artist. He also sells real estate. He's carrying a few of his paintings under his arm: watercolors. He shows me.

The paintings are mostly of people, in shades of brown and gray and blue. Muted tones, he calls them. The people are standing around like sticks in a wash of dirty purple on what looks like it could be a street somewhere. Or maybe a parking lot. They all have their heads bowed, as if from exhaustion, or it could be shame. Maybe they're on the verge of sleep. The whole scene reminds me weirdly of a garden in early winter, the people left over like dead flowers or corn stalks, and I wonder whether that's what he's trying to say. He must have six or seven paintings like this, all variations on the same theme. Depressing. But I tell him it's interesting, which in a way it is.

I watch him as he heads up the stairs to Brenda's studio. I might find it in me to be a little jealous, but there's no denying Ted's a nice guy. What does bother me a little, I guess, is that Brenda shows him her paintings, sometimes even before they're finished. That's an artist-to-artist sort of thing, I suppose. I don't know, maybe I should have taken up painting, instead of reading poetry. Though that might seem a bit transparent. I'm of the opinion, where Brenda is concerned, an oblique approach is best.

Later on, over dinner, the time seems right. I ask Brenda about Ted's paintings, what she thinks of them.

She pauses over a forkful of mussel. "What, he showed them to you?"

"Yeah, when he came over today. Why? You sound surprised."

"Well, I am, a little. Normally he's very sensitive about his work."

Grinning, I'm gazing into my wife's eyes. "Then he must have recognized in me an unusually receptive soul."

Brenda's perfect lips close over the mussel, and the fork comes away clean.

I feel an urge right now for an act of impudence. I'd like to get my tongue into her mouth to steal that mussel she believes is hers. I'd like to pick her up, kick her chair over, and lay her out on the white table cloth. Dinner can wait.

Brenda is silent. Her eyes sparkle while they seem to assess me. Slowly she nods. "Could you pass the herb salt?" she says finally.

When the phone rings, Brenda is up to answer it.

I hear her from the kitchen. "Oh, hi, Sybil." There is a pause. Then, "Uh-huh. Oh, no. No. No, I haven't." Her voice seems increasingly heavy, commiserative. Sybil is a neighbor, somewhat high-strung. She lives two properties down from us.

I'm sitting at our walnut diningroom table, gazing at Brenda's empty walnut chair. I'm wondering idly what Brenda now knows that I don't know.

She returns, sits. She shakes her head. "That was Sybil. Desdemona has disappeared."

"Who?"

"Desdemona. Her cat?"

"Oh."

I'm no particular friend of cats. It takes a moment for it to register: for a certain kind of person, the disappearance of a cat can be a matter of some gravity.

Brenda says, "Something has gotten into their trash, too, lately. She's worried it could be a dog."

"Ah."

Brenda takes possession of her wine glass, leans back in her chair. She runs her hand through her hair, a gesture of consummation. She's finished with dinner.

"Or some wild animal," Brenda says, shaking her head. "Sybil's imagination runs away with these things."

She says the word "wild" with a certain emphatic flare. I'm convinced I'll never in my life see a more beautiful woman.

I'm sitting there, damp-eyed, watching her, my fingers wrapped around the herb salt.

THE WOMAN in gray. Try as I might, I can't stop thinking about her. How did she come to be there in our yard? And why in the world was she staring up into my window? Some sort of robe, she seemed to be wearing. Otherwise all I remember are her eyes. Fifty feet away—she might as well have been right next to me. I've never, ever had anyone look at me like that. The incident has stirred something in me that I haven't felt in years. Not since we left the city.

To begin with, you just don't find people walking around Brandewoode. Cars, of course. Once in a while a motorcycle. Even now and then a bicycle—for exercise, not transportation. But not once, in the five years we've lived here, have I come across anyone on foot. Not once.

The only person I've told so far is Stan. He was no help at all.

Lately, the fact is, I've been a bit worried about Stan. His wife, Alice, left him a couple of years ago. They owned one of the finest homes in Brandewoode. Stan used to be devoted to the place. You'd hear about him outside, laying stone walls. He even built himself a barn, designed the thing himself, which put the neighbors a bit on edge. These days, though, he's hardly ever home. I don't know what he does with himself or where he goes, out maybe to some water hole. And now—I don't know if this is coincidence—Stan has a new girlfriend. Dolores. She works in the Argus Towers Snack bar. I haven't actually seen her, but news gets around.

Dolores is a single mom and has green hair. I just hope Stan knows what he's doing.

Anyway, when I told him about the woman in gray, Stan was hunched over the table by my window, straightening a paperclip, giving it his full attention. But as soon as I mentioned the woman, he glanced up. He looked at me funny.

"What?" I said.

"You're not going to tell me she had that face."

"What face?"

"The one in your dream."

"No, no, this wasn't the dream. Listen, she was right there on our lawn. I was wide awake."

"Did anyone else see her?"

"No, she was in our back yard for Christ sake."

Stan said, "I had a dream the other night where everyone spoke in bar codes."

Sonya's voice piped up from the outer office, "I had one like that!"

"Hey, if you people want to talk about dreams," I said, "go right ahead. I won't stop you."

Stan was silent for a minute. Then he said, "What did she look like?—this woman in gray."

"I don't know. I couldn't really see much of her all wrapped up like that."

He nodded, evidently giving it some thought. Then he said, "Who knows? I think you might have something there."

"What do you mean?"

"You never know. I'd say it's a promising omen, at the very least."

It seemed I wasn't getting my point across. I said, "If we could get rid of some of those weeds . . . ."

"Weeds? What is it about you and weeds?"

"At the edge of our yard. I tried getting Swenson to cut them down, but he wouldn't do it."

"The hell with Swenson. Look, I have a machete you're welcome to borrow. If weeds are your problem."

"Yeah, I think that's how she was able to sneak out of the woods."

"Wait a minute." Stan looked at me intently. "You're cutting down weeds to get rid of the woman in the robe?"

THE FOLLOWING Sunday morning I'm out golfing with Vince. The two of us are standing on the sixth tee, waiting in the mist, in case the players ahead of us haven't finished. Vince now and then squints in the direction of the green. If the air were any wetter, we'd be underwater. Vince probably knows, but I can't remember, how long this hole is—whether, if we tee off now, we might bean somebody. I'm not about to make the first move.

The ground is pretty spongy where we're standing. The drizzle is starting to form little droplets on my eyelashes—I can see them. As to what I think about this game called *golf*, I haven't decided one way or the other. It's nice enough on a sunny day. Then again, what isn't? But I find it hard saying no to Vince when it comes to certain things.

Never mind the discomfort. In this weather, the main trouble is keeping track of the ball. A couple of weeks ago Vince got fed up with it and bought a pack of neon-colored balls. We've been using those. I wind up with pink usually, or yellow. Vince keeps the orange balls for himself. Still I can't say that it has made a lot of difference.

Now, finally, Vince says, "Why don't you hit."

I tee up, then pause (purely out of habit) for what's supposed to be a canny assessment of the green. Naturally I can't *see* the green. What the hell, I address the ball and whack it. Like a little raspberry-colored comet, it zings out over the grass. By the time it burrows its way into the mist, it has already begun to slice. At least, with the ground this saturated, it shouldn't roll far.

Now Vince tees and hits a straight shot, low, mandarin orange, headed right down the fairway until it, too, disappears into the mist. We grab our carts and start for the green.

I have no easy time locating the ball. A few hundred feet and, looking back, I can't see the tee anymore. I'm walking the right-hand border of the fairway, trying to stay oriented. Features of the landscape loom and fade. I've lost track of the spot where the ball disappeared. Somewhere off to my left Vince is waiting for me to hit so he can go ahead. Conscious of this, I scour the rough in ever-widening circles. My shoes and the hem of my pants are soaked. The entire time, for no good reason, I'm keeping an eye out for snakes. There's a certain slithery feel to the air.

Finally I spot the little gleam of pink in a hollow behind a small bush. I call to Vince, who yells go ahead and hit for Christ's sake. I'm ready to knock it out into the open where I can get a decent shot at it, but I'm having trouble focusing. The truth is I don't care about the damn ball because there's something else going on. Behind me in the fog, it's becoming obvious, there's something there. I'm certain of this. I spin around. The mists swirl, closing in over the vertical smudges of tree trunks, a whole line of them standing alongside the fairway like dark ghosts.

It shouldn't be a big deal, a line of trees. But they don't look familiar. My blood is racing.

I call out to Vince, "Hey, are there trees along this fairway?"

I hear his voice, impatient. "Hit for God's sake, will you?"

So I go back to my ball, kick it into the open. Still, I keep looking over my shoulder. I hit out with a five-iron. Not a bad shot, at least what little I can see of it. Back toward where I saw the trees, there's no sign of anything.

Vince is on the green in three. I'm right at the edge in, strictly speaking, five or six, but I tell him four. Vince putts away, then plants the flag back in the hole and stands there holding it while I evaluate my lie. Let's see. There is my pink, dimpled ball. There is fifteen, eighteen feet of green, deceptively contoured and damp. There's the hole with the pin in it. And there are Vince's trousers and his golf shoes—whether I like it or not, definitely part of the equation. I wish he had just left the flag where it was.

By the time I finally make my putt, I've lost track of the number of strokes. The ball rattles into the hole. I say, "Well, it took me long enough."

I glance up then to see Vince staring at me, but not the way I expected. Not the familiar fatherly stare, the stare of forborne disappointment. No, this is far worse, this flicker of hollowness across his face. It's as if, behind those eyes, there is finally nothing, except possibly the urge to tear me limb from limb.

I pull the scorecard, dog-eared, out of my pocket, as if this might be the thing to fend him off. I back away, jotting down the numbers. "Jeez, Vince, you're killing me," I say. I'm aware of his bulk, stock still, out of the corner of my eye.

He chuckles then, and I see him shake his head and grin. The old Vince.

As we're pulling our carts along to the seventh tee, he still has that grin on his face as if, try as he might, he can't shake it.

Afterward, we stop at his place and sit outside on his patio with gin and tonics, lime wedges on the rims of the glasses. Birds fidget in the apple tree overhead. Vince tells me he planted the tree with his own hands, fifteen years ago. The patio, which he also put in, is partly enclosed by a wall and bordered by grapevines and rose hedges. In fact, most of the trees and flowers we can see Vince planted himself. He won't let Swenson near them. The guy takes his yard seriously.

I wouldn't tell Vince this, but the goddamned yard looks almost too good to be real.

It's pleasant enough sitting there, though, after a disconcerting morning on the links. I still don't know what to make of it. Maybe, after all, Stan has a point. Maybe sometimes I make things more difficult than they need to be.

Later, when I'm pulling into our driveway, I have to stop momentarily for Ted, who's just leaving. He waves, and I wave back, each from our car windows.

After I turn off the ignition, I sit in the car, listening to the engine cool down by little metallic ticks. I don't think about anything. I just sit.

An Excess of Happiness

THE PORCH DOOR fits so tightly against its frame, it looks not like an actual entrance but like a painting of one. The morning, apparently just arrived, waits now around this door in an expectant half-circle.

The back yard has undergone a change from weeks ago. Its brilliant green stillness no longer overwhelms, but seems rather now a prelude to something else—something a bit like autumn. But not autumn. Something else. The lawn and gardens are tarnished about the edges. Flowers weigh heavily on their stalks. Among the bushes and branches of the trees, song sparrows chatter and flit energetically. The sparrows are flocking, barely pausing here on their flight south. Hopping from twig to twig, turning themselves this way and that, they eye the porch door as if with skepticism.

The air brightens a little, tinting the fog yellow, the sun perhaps for a moment gaining strength. Then again, perhaps not.

Now with a squeak the porch door swings open, and he emerges, capturing the attention of the sparrows, who instantly freeze. As the door bangs closed, he pauses for a measured glance in the direction of the woods, then quickly descends the steps. He carries in one hand a briefcase and in the other a white plastic kitchen bag bloated with the trash and the air trapped inside. His movements seem hurried, automatic, until the sight of the trash cans stops him on the flagstones.

There on the concrete next to the cans, a couple of bulging black plastic bags tilt at opposing angles. One bag has been opened, its contents spilled over the walk and the lawn. He steps closer, his mouth falling open. The white plastic bag drops from his hand as he squats, reaches, and grabs the end of a broken chain threaded through the handles on the cans and one of the lids. A second lid—he now discovers—lies, like a gigantic tossed coin, maybe fifty feet away in the middle of the lawn.

    He sets his briefcase aside. The chain rattles as he pulls it taut against its anchor in the concrete, then tests it with a couple of vigorous tugs. He picks up a snapped chain link lying on the walk by his shoes and studies it, turning it over and over in his fingers. Slowly he rises to stare at the clapboards above the trash cans, where a small key hangs by a nail.

    But finally, it seems, it is the forest that really interests him. All the while he is retrieving the can lid from the lawn, he never once takes his eyes off the tree line bordering the yard.

    Back at the ravaged trash cans, he stoops and scrapes up the mess with the lid, dumping it back into the open bag. He works quickly, glancing over his shoulder continually at the woods, but at the last clump he pauses. It looks like next to nothing, a folded wad of damp Kleenex. But it stops him. He examines it, using the broken chain link to gingerly pick it apart. Then he holds entirely still. For a long moment he does nothing. He is half-kneeling, bent over, staring at the soggy lump in the trash can lid.

    What is he looking at?

    The sparrows are in motion again, migrating like static along the edge of the woods. Bird particles, abandoning oak twigs, leapfrog through the rhododendron. They are so many, and their eyes seem to take in everything at once. It could be the air they're interested in, studying it from different angles. In any event they take no notice of this one thing in the trash can lid, which has turned this man into a statue.

    It seems they already know about it. It seems they long ago had their fill of it.

I'M STANDING HERE, facing this wall. Absurd, yes, but true. The wall, with its delicate floral pattern, is the perfect insult. The perfect mockery. The end of things. Some mistake, somewhere. Oh, God. How? How?

There must have been a bad mistake. And then it just unraveled. Somewhere it all came apart. But where? I don't see it.

I don't know what else. I'm holding my fist, all set to go, inches from this wall. Inches from this light switch. I'm prepared to break the bones of my hand. I'm ready to open myself up, ready to bleed. Honestly, I don't know what else.

Somewhere. Somewhere there must be a thread. Something to take me back. To the point where I could have made a difference. Where I could have stopped it in its tracks. Or am I just kidding myself? Were the seeds of this nightmare there from the beginning?

God.

Jesus Mary, mother. Son of a bitch.

There, just listen to me. Vomiting out these pathetic vulgarities, these stupid secondhand blasphemies. That's about all that there is in my arsenal. Michael's Counteroffensive.

Yes. So right now I'm reduced to spitting—that's right— spitting on the carpet, trying to rid myself of the torture of this helplessness. Trying to excrete my own impotence. I'm ready to pick up one of these goddamned diningroom chairs and crack this silly walnut table in half. This table, God, this altar of our evening communion. But no. Even this would be insufficient. Even this would amount to nothing.

    I don't know where to go from here. I don't.

    This pain, like a spear wound. For hours now, it must be, I've been walking around in circles, around in circles, literally, like a madman. I could do anything right now. I tell you, I'm capable of just about anything. Anything—except, of course, whatever would make a difference. That's where Michael comes up short.

    What remains of my life I simply have no words for.

    Well, O.K., it's true. It is. About all that's left is the awful truth of this. My Brenda. She has been having an affair. My Brenda.

    Impossible. But nonetheless true. Another man has been enjoying my wife. Another man. And I have to assume the enjoyment has been mutual.

    I haven't slept, I don't know how long it's been. It doesn't matter. The morning . . . the day before yesterday, I think, I found out. Or the day before that. And ever since then there has been this . . . firestorm inside me. Which is a good way of putting it. A firestorm, where everything is white hot, so that you can't even look at things. And where everything is consumed. Nothing is spared.

    So I haven't been able to think clearly. In fact I haven't been able to think at all.

    But eventually out of the ashes it does become possible once again to look at things, if not to actually see them. And, when I do, there it is, practically the only thing left standing: my wife's infidelity.

    Brenda's. Infidelity.

    But actually that isn't quite everything. There is also something else. Something underlying all of this, and just now seeping to the surface. The truth is I've suspected for awhile. Though until this moment I haven't admitted it.

    Yes. I have suspected.

The change, I believe, began some time ago. Last year maybe, or—now that I think about it—the year before. The sense that something had been overlooked. I'd forgotten all about that.

Right now I'm imagining being granted my wish. I'm imagining traveling back in time to a much purer air. Back, long before that moment of discovery. Yes, back before then, to a time when I still could have done something.
But what?
What could I have done?
I would, if I were going back, have to think about that, very carefully.

A year or two ago? Or maybe three? It's true. A certain distance developed between us. We discovered, Brenda and I, lighter, more artful ways of speaking. I remember it seemed a good thing at the time, almost a form of flirtation. Lively discussions bubbled between us. We debated whether or not we should eat every evening at the diningroom table. Whether the lighting of candles was essential to that experience. Did we think the color of the walls required a shade more warmth? Was I buying my trousers too short? Of course, in the light of what has come to pass, these questions now appear trivial, if not actually grotesque.
I have to wonder, where was Brenda then, really? And where was I?
We became, perhaps, too comfortable with one another—and then, as a result of that, not comfortable at all. No, not even in bed. Regardless of what I might have said earlier.
No, to be perfectly honest, it was as if the very air between us had hardened. Sometimes she would talk, and I would hold onto that talk—not what she was saying because I don't think she intended to say anything really. It was her voice I wanted, that part of her. And then, in time, even that was stilled. Just the two of us

lying there, as though under an increase in the force of gravity. Lying there, maybe our eyes blinking.

It's all so clear now. All so clear. Yet for two years and more, I was living the life of a blind man. And now, now that I have eyes, it seems there is nothing at all to see.

WEIRD. I'd almost forgotten about our trash. That indispensable commodity. It's in high demand, apparently, around the neighborhood, compared to other people's trash. That latest episode—the broken chain, the can lid tossed aside like a frisbee. What am I supposed to make of that?

Once upon a time, that sort of nonsense would have been a big deal. It would have rankled, yes, the fact that every other week in the dead of night, while we were asleep in bed, some deranged being was stalking out of the woods for the single purpose of rearranging our garbage. This would have actually mattered—I don't know why. Back then, it seems, there couldn't have been a lot going on around here, if that was the item topping the agenda. Right now I've got real things to worry about, like what I'm going to do about my wife.

I should do something, right? I can't just let it sit like this.

After I first found out, I was sick, on my back in bed, for days. I was running a fever of 102.5. Brenda, ironically, played the part of the angel. She brought me soup and sandwiches on a tray, the sandwiches cut diagonally, the way women know how to cut them. I couldn't eat a crumb. The sight of her was torture.

Here it is two weeks later. She still doesn't suspect that I know. What am I waiting for?

The two of us pass one another. We inhabit the same rooms—always on the verge, it seems, but never connecting. We move, trapped in this ghost constellation, like planets that have somehow eluded their suns. I used to think I loved my wife. Who was it that I loved? I observe Brenda's behavior now as if from behind a one-way mirror. I see what she doesn't know I see, what she believes is invisible. The same as before, I suppose, in a way. But also different.

There's been another break-in at ZACTRON. I can't make head nor tails of it—other than that the miscreant, whoever he is, made off with another sixteen employees. I work at rearranging their last initials. This time they spell *Michael loves Sta*n. I read the message again, and then again, feeling tiny pinpricks at my temples, under my arms, on the back of my neck.

Half an hour later I show Stan.

His jaw tightens. "This does not look good," he says.

"No kidding. It's like the firewall doesn't exist."

"It's what happens when you depend on firewalls. By now he's probably put in a back door."

"Not that I could find. What's he up to anyway? He's in, bang—he grabs the names, and he's gone."

Stan is already at the keyboard. He doesn't say anything. He works on it for ten or fifteen minutes while I watch.

"O.K.," he says finally. "IDS hasn't seen a trace of him. No bacteria, no rabbits, no bombs. Whatever he's packing in he's packing out. I'd say he's just having himself a good time."

"So the *Michael* and *Stan*," I say. "This has to be one of our own, right?"

Stan hasn't stopped typing. He shakes his head, but in a way that I think means yes.

I offer to go for coffee. He doesn't say anything. I go anyway. The sitting around and waiting is driving me crazy.

When I get back with the coffee, Stan has stopped typing. He is just sitting there, staring at the screen, as if deep in thought.

I hand him the coffee.

He pushes himself away from my desk, stands, and goes to the window. He's sipping coffee, staring out the window. He might be hatching some grand solution.

"Cattle," he says. "They want to turn us all into cattle."

"What do you mean?"

He ignores my question. His voice sounds distant, wistful. "A couple of weeks ago, on the way home, I saw this road."

The silence blares.

"What road?"

He turns to me. "Hm?"

"What road? You said you'd seen a road."

Stan shrugs. "Oh, I don't know. Somewhere off 17." He slurps his coffee.

"What kind of road?"

Stan is standing, staring in the direction of the computer screen. "It's the truth," he says. "I'm afraid what this boils down to here is we've got human issues."

I nod.

Stan says, "Either they're red-teaming us. Or someone in here has turned to the dark side."

I'm nodding. I'm looking at the computer screen because it seems that, since I'm agreeing with him, that's where I should be looking.

I don't know how much time passes. A few seconds, probably. I say, "What kind of road?"

Stan looks at me.

"You mentioned just now that you'd seen a road. Off 17."

"I don't know. Just some road. Winding up into the heather. I'd never seen it before." His voice has that distant quality again. He sips his coffee. His eyes drift back to the computer screen. "There was something about it."

There has been a change.

I am tormented by dreams. I think they're dreams.

Where I am, it's just another starless night in a life of starless nights. I'm up on a stone building. I'm on the roof, teetering right at the edge. This building, I have no idea what it is, but I am aware that it is filled with torment. My need to get off the roof is clear, but there is no going that way, back in through the building. From the darkness, on the other hand, I feel an increasing magnetism, a little like the sound of my own name. Its attraction pulls at my limbs and at my neck. I'm standing there, right at the edge, mesmerized by the weight of all that starlessness. I'm leaning, inching forward, this longing within my throat.

 I believe I haven't slept in a long time.

 The dreams come anyway.

·

 What I really, really don't understand is the Ted part. I'd never in my life have expected treachery from that corner. Never. All right, I can see the logic of it, her going for another painter. But Ted? This perfect sweetheart? I've never seen more genuine eye contact. The guy showed me his paintings, for Christ's sake!

 Of course, I don't know for a fact it's Ted. He can't be the only painter around. That class she attends so religiously must be filled with them. Not to mention the instructor. With the dark hair and the holes in his sweatshirt. What's his name—Conner. First name or last name, I have no idea. From the start, I didn't like the look of him. I'm walking around the living room now thinking about him, I've got a golf club in my hand. A nine iron. This is not good.

 Not that it matters, really, *who* it is.

 I'm serious, though. There really has been a change.

 For one thing, I'm still reading poetry. I don't know what it is, I can't give it up. You'd expect present circumstances would have sucked the motivation right out of me. There's no need, obviously, to impress Brenda anymore. Still I keep turning the pages. Right now it's James Wright. At my desk, in my study, here in the dead of night. Brenda's in bed, asleep long ago. And I'm up reading James, with a kind of fever. My arms and my hands holding the book feel electric. I couldn't put him down if I wanted to. The moments float out of these poems. Again and again, the words bring everything to a standstill.

Of course I have to wonder, this world he's in touch with—James—where is it? Has he made the place up, Martin's Ferry, entirely out of words? Or is it still lying, somewhere west of here, actual and flat under a somewhat yellow light.?

For a moment there, I was tempted to say dawdling light. I don't know why. There is a certain animal readiness to these urges.

I look up from the page and stare out into the night. It's quiet, but not entirely quiet. I do hear something out there, I'm not sure what—frogs maybe, or crickets. And . . . some sort of rustling. Even such simple goings-on, I know so little!

The darkness out there seems just about limitless. It's enough to sap the will out of you. The world is brimful of it, this darkness. At night now, mists obliterating the sky, I feel it flooding in, washing through the confusion of trees in these woods, lapping right up against the clapboard walls of this house.

What I've been trying to say is there really has been a change. Maybe I'm even closer to understanding it, this . . . something. And now, exactly this moment, with a suddenness that is like waking up, I realize—whatever it is—it's downstairs! Inside the house, downstairs.

How it got in I have no idea. The entrances are locked. I haven't heard any noise. It's the middle of the night.

I close James Wright and slip the book onto my desk. I'm careful not to make a sound. I stand and, with a remarkable lack of hesitation, pick up my chair—it's the only weapon I can lay my hands on. I position myself just inside the doorway to my study. I'm so perfectly quiet, not even a floorboard creaks.

There's enough light in the hall outside that I'll have a clear view of whoever passes. Brenda at this moment is lying in the next room, defenseless in her nightclothes. I wait, the chair raised over my head. I listen for the familiar squeak of the stairs. Or for something else, anything. I wait a long time—it must be ten minutes, or more—until the muscles of my back and arms are shot with pain. Then, just as I'm about to shift position, I hear the front door click shut.

I poke my head out into the hallway. It's completely empty. Where I'm standing, I can see clear down the stairs almost to the front door. From the bedroom, just down the hall, I hear Brenda give a little groan in her sleep. That's the only sound. In the air there is a trace of an odor, something I'm not familiar with. Something I can't remember ever having smelled before.

Out in the hall I set the chair down on the carpet. I'm not sure what to do. Whoever, or whatever, it was downstairs seems to be gone, though I can't be certain about this. I sit. It occurs to me that if Brenda were to awaken now and see me like this, apparently watching at the top of the stairs, it would be hard for me to explain myself. But so what? Brenda can go ahead and ask all the questions she wants. If it comes to that, I have a few of my own.

I'm going over it all in my head. All the lessons. I've learned how easily a yard can be violated. And a place of employment. And a marriage. And now a home. That too. What next?

I'M IN THE CHECKOUT LINE at the liquor store when I spot Ted in the next line over, charming the woman next to him with his senseless banter. I'm weirdly fascinated by the sight of him—I'd love to put his lights out. He stoops and hefts a case of wine from his cart onto the counter by the register. A Pinot grigio. Then a second case. A Bordeaux. Both of them on sale. Grunting with the effort, he doesn't make it look easy. His arms are nothing like Swenson's. I watch Ted's every move. Of course, anyone can see he's the kind women go for. Still, I'm wondering.

I look quickly away, my gaze passing over my own purchases—three liters of Bombay and a 750 of indifferent vermouth—before coming to rest on the automaton-like movements of my bagger, a young man with a Mohawk, an earring, and acne.

I overhear Ted joking with his cashier—something, it seems, about the weather. And then his bagger gets into the act, the three of them chuckling heartily.

Preoccupied with my credit card transaction, I feel perfectly comfortable ignoring all of this. I sign the receipt. The cashier hands me my copy, and my attention returns to my lethargic bagger, his head drooping as if from exhaustion, or it could be embarrassment. As I watch him sheathe my vermouth in paper, he takes me in with an ambiguous stare.

But then I don't have to look at him either. I'm far enough along that I can plausibly interest myself in the parking lot, where I'm headed next. And actually there is something striking about the scene out there. I'm trying to think what it reminds me of. In the seepage of purple-gray light, several people are standing around, oddly derelict. You might think they were searching for something, the way their heads are bowed. Except that they're all motionless. It's a little unnerving, seeing them that way, lifeless as corn stalks in some winter garden. The more I look, the less I like it.

In fact, I don't see why I need to waste any more time here. On my way out of the store I can still hear Ted's voice. Against my better instincts, I glance his way, and of course his eyes latch onto me. He gives me a two-fingered wave and a big smile. And then, sure enough, a wink.

Even out in the car, after I've had a chance to calm down a bit, my heart is pounding.

I've brought James Wright down to the dinner table. What the hell. After my run-in earlier with Ted, I feel ready for an act of open rebellion. I'm reading from *The Green Wall*, turning the pages with my left hand, forking salad into my mouth with my right.

If Brenda notices, she doesn't show any sign of it. She says, "I've been on the phone again with Sybil."

I make a "hmph!" sound. I don't look up from my reading. "What's bothering her now? Another cat gone missing?"

Hearing nothing from Brenda, I glance up to see her looking at me. She has hardly touched her meal.

"What?" I say.

"Both of Sybil's cats are dead."

"What do you mean 'dead'?"

"As in 'not alive.' Clayton Bresnahan found them this morning, on the lawn next to his bird feeder."

"Dead? So what happened to them?"

"They don't know yet. The police took the animals as evidence, sealed them up in plastic bags. They're running tests on them."

"Tests. On cats."

"They stopped by this morning, the police. They went through the entire neighborhood, questioning everybody. It seems they think there may have been a witness."

"Why do they think that?"

"I don't know. They're police."

"Strange. Did you tell them about our trash?"

"What about it?"

"That nut case, the one who's been messing with our garbage. Maybe he killed the cats."

"That seems a bit far-fetched, doesn't it?"

Through the diningroom window I hear, somewhere in the back yard, the unmistakable squeak of a wheelbarrow. I'm calculating. Sybil's house is only five doors down from ours. If it weren't for the woods being in the way, we'd probably be able to see her back door right from our porch. I'm wondering whether our doors are locked.

Brenda says, "Then around noon, Brandewoode Security appeared at the door. There were three or four of them. They went all over the grounds, combing the edge of the woods."

"*Our* grounds?"

"Everybody's. All the homes on Forest Drive."

Out in the yard a shovel is scraping, rasping against a wheelbarrow. I say, "Is that Swenson out there?" I'm craning my neck, but I can't see him. "Why's he working so late?"

"I don't know." Brenda shrugs. "He seemed in a bad mood today. I think Security got a bit in his way, taking up his time with questions, stomping over his gardens."

For the moment, I set James Wright aside, put my fork down. "Wow," I say.

"Poor Sybil. She can barely talk."

For once, I can sympathize with the woman. I say, "Who knows, though. There's probably a simple explanation. Maybe they ate some poisoned mice or something."

Brenda directs her gaze out the window to the gray-green of the yard, where the evening light is growing dimmer by the second. She says, "Honestly I thought, when we moved here, we were done with this sort of thing."

The ominous tone in her voice catches me off guard. I don't like being reminded of the city.

She spears a broccoli flower with her fork. "Odd to think whoever it is might still be out there. *You* haven't seen anyone lurking around, have you?"

"No. What do you mean? Why would I?"

"Well, gee, Michael." She looks at me. "No need to be defensive."

The Saturday morning following, I notice Swenson out in the yard pruning the shrubbery along the border by the woods. I have an uncontrollable urge to ask him about the big event. The mysterious cat murders. Brenda doesn't want to talk about it. When I questioned Stan, who lives less than a mile away, he hadn't even heard about it. But Swenson should know plenty.

Between the downstairs bathroom, laundry room, and kitchen, I scrounge enough trash to carry out to the cans. On my way out I let the door slam. At the cans, I rattle the lid. Then I look over, as though just noticing him.

"Hey, Swenson," I say, "how's it going?" I approach him.

He looks up then, employing a motion of his head that could be construed as a gesture of recognition, or not.

"Hey," I say, in no mood to beat around the bush, "you haven't seen any large animals around here, have you?"

He suspends the act of pruning and gives me a questioning look.

"You know," I say, "it's the damnedest thing. We've had something after our trash lately."

"Yah?"

"Yeah. Just plain refuses to leave it alone. Won't take no for an answer, whatever it is. It's weird."

"Hah," he says.

"Yeah. As a matter of fact, it got so bad, last week I fastened the lids down with a chain, threw a lock on the whole damn thing. Hung the key right on the house there."

He tilts his head at that. The key seems to have impressed him.

"And what do you think," I say, "it broke the chain."

"Hah." Swenson shakes his head.

"Just snapped it right in two."

"Yah," he says. He goes back to pruning. "It don't surprise me." He stoops and lops a branch off at the base of the hedge.

"No?"

"Nah."

I'll have to wait to find out why not.

He snips off another branch then pauses. "It's kids," he says.

"Kids?"

"Yah."

"You think kids could break a chain like that?"

He chuckles. "Oh, yah. Easy."

It's a comforting thought somehow, that that's all it might be, just a little overflow of teenage testosterone. But I don't believe it for a minute. "Hm!" I say.

"Yah. Easy."

Each branch that Swenson removes from the hedge he drops at his feet onto a small but accumulating bundle of snipped branches, all arranged parallel, their butt ends pointing in the same direction. I can't pretend to be interested in this for very long. "Oh, by the way," I say, "did you hear what happened to Mrs. Monroe's cats?"

"Ho!" His eyes grow wide.

"I can't imagine kids are responsible for that." I no sooner say it than I begin to doubt it. These so-called kids, let's face it, can be awfully malicious.

But on this point Swenson seems to agree. "That there's the work of a devil," he says.

"Right," I say tentatively. "Yeah."

But I don't like the way he's looking at me. After all, it's not as though I had anything to do with it.

"What do you think?" I say. "Do the police have any idea who it was?"

He sneers. "The police."

"Did they talk to you?"

"Yah, they talk. Of course. The police, they're good at talking. Not so good at listening."

"True. Yeah."

"They think they know it all, the police. Drive in the patrol cars, knock on the doors, they think they know everything." He snips another branch, lays it neatly on the pile. "But there's plenty they don't know."

"Yeah? Like what?"

He chuckles, points a finger at the ground. "A man stands out here in the open air, he'll see some things. The police, let them knock on all the doors they want. What are they going to see? Not what's here. Not what's in these woods."

"Hm!" I say.

Conversations with Swenson can tend to wander a bit. And I'm already losing track of what we're talking about, Swenson and I. Out in front of the house, I think I hear a car door slam. Maybe Brenda leaving, or someone arriving. It could even be Ted. I listen for an engine starting.

Taking a step backward, I glance down at the pile of pruned branches. "So you plan on burning these?"

"Burning?" Swenson holds me in an incredulous stare. "There's a ban in force. These, hell, they go to the compost."

I'm about to ask, what ban?—given that this is the most drizzly autumn on record. If autumn is what you want to call it. But I do hear a car now, so, taking my leave of Swenson, I hurry around to the front of the house. By the time I get there, Brenda's car is down the driveway, turning onto Forest Drive.

And now, as if I haven't got enough problems, it seems someone has been messing with my golf clubs. I'll leave the bag in the right-hand corner of the garage, and it will wind up instead in the left-hand corner. Or I'll find the seven-iron out on the lawn. Or the number-three wood in the driveway, where I could easily run over it.

I ask Brenda about it. She gives me a look that says, in effect, "What in the world would I want with your golf clubs?"

Which leaves Swenson. Unless the Trash Marauder has a hand in it. Either way, I'm not expecting an explanation soon.

I MARVEL at Suzanne, who produces almost no sound moving from her desk to her filing cabinets and back again. She has work enough to keep her busy, but she doesn't waste motion. It's impossible not to watch her. My marriage in ruins, I feel more and more defenseless that way around women.

"Would you like coffee?" Her voice, muffled by the pile of the carpet, seems to come from the window, though I'm looking straight at her. She smiles generously, the smile rippling into little smile aftertremors, each one of them charged—I'm tempted to believe—with meaning. I readily accept the coffee even though my hands are jittery from the several cups I've already put away this morning. I wouldn't know how to say no to her.

I take the cup with two hands, both my thumbs twitching. She pretends, I suspect, not to notice.

Suzanne is Jack Folsom's secretary. I'm supposed to have a meeting with Jack, though I have to say it feels more like an appointment. This is just another example. I'm losing track of the order of things around here. Lately everything at Argus seems to be shifting. You can never be sure anymore whether you're on solid ground. Maybe I'm here to answer questions about the repeated ZACTRON break-ins, but that's only a guess.

As if she has been reading my thoughts, Suzanne turns to me and smiles again reassuringly.

There is no reassurance whatever in Jack's expression, nor anywhere else in this room he calls his office. It's not like any other office I've ever been in. The place is laid out with exceptional taste, an oriental rug centered on its hardwood floor. On the wall to my right, next to a door, hang a couple of what I imagine to be Peruvian blankets, a deep, rich red. The furniture is stylish, probably European-manufactured. On one of the pieces, a small table by the window, he's set a sculpture in dark wood: a primitive-looking figure bent into a contorted pose, staring with one of those eerie faces. Once upon a time, the sculpture—the size of a small dog—might have had religious significance, but these days it's the kind of thing you might see in a museum. The overall effect in the room is strangely spare, not at all overdone. Brenda, I cannot help thinking, would approve.

Jack has been standing, I don't know how long now, his attention apparently fastened on a single sheet of paper on his desk. I've taken the sofa against the wall, the spot Jack seemed to indicate, though I may have committed an error by sitting sooner than appropriate. The five fingertips of Jack's right hand rest on the edge of his desktop. He looks like a man who has just this moment struck a piano chord, and a fairly dramatic one at that.

I lift the styrofoam cup to my lips and pretend to sip. Then, lowering the cup, I pretend to see something of interest out the window, where in fact nothing is visible beyond the whitish gray oblivion of the fog.

Jack hasn't budged. His fingertips seem now, if anything, even more firmly planted on the surface of his desk, as if he might be about to levitate.

"Vince," he says finally. "Vince."

I hesitate. "I'm Michael."

Jack closes his eyes, his fingers pinching the bridge of his nose. He says, "Let's talk about Vince."

"Vince Marconi."

"I'd like your impression. You've worked under Vince for some time?"

"Four years now. You want my impression of him?"

Jack opens his eyes. He finds his chair and sits.

I don't like where this is headed. "Vince," I say, ". . . well, I don't know, I hardly feel qualified . . ."

Jack purses his lips.

Leaning reflectively back against the couch, my eyes hunting the ceiling for inspiration, I'm hoping to come up with what, on some level, amounts to an answer. But there's a distraction. Some odd sound.

Jack is staring straight at me. There is an unpleasantness about his eyes.

I try again. "I mean I've learned an awful lot from Vince, I really have. The guy's depth of experience. He has a pretty impressive history here."

"History," Jack says, his voice flat. "You want to talk about history." He reaches, scoops a book off the corner of his desk. He opens it, flips a few pages, shuts it again. He smiles. "These days, Michael, what it boils down to is *economies of readiness*. And we'd better be prepared to accept what that means."

"Well, . . ."

"Look, Michael. You strike me—correct me if I'm wrong—as a man with his eye on the horizon."

I'm nodding, as if this seems not an unreasonable characterization.

But there is something else, interfering. That noise. Not one you'd expect in an office. Not, say, the sound of a copy machine or the buzz of fluorescent lighting or even the roll of a file cabinet drawer. Nothing like any of those.

Jack says, "We have to think more expansively, Michael. Picture Argus going forward, say five years, ten years from now. What do you see?" He tosses the book back onto his desktop, clasps his hands over his stomach. I have his undivided attention.

It shouldn't be difficult. I should be able to answer him. But that sound keeps nagging, getting in the way. It's a little like sandpaper. Like steam escaping from something. But with a dangerous undertone—like, say, the hum of electronic equipment. Only magnified.

How is it, anyway, that I've come to be here? One day a blinding fog moves in. Something is pilfering my trash. Before I know it, they've dragged me in for interrogation in what looks like a hotel lobby. And then this sound. Coming, it seems now, from behind the door by the Peruvian wall hangings, the door opposite the one I entered by. A soft, breathy sound. Respiratory, you could call it. But . . . yes, electronic. I can even smell it. I'm sitting more or less hypnotized by it, until I hear Jack's chair creak.

Have I given him an answer yet? Maybe it doesn't matter, the way he's barging ahead. "Enterprise vulnerability management solutions," he's saying. "That's what we provide. Science has nothing to do with it. It's an art. And we've become deadly efficient at it. It is the reason our customers are willing to dig into their pockets and hand over portions of their hard-earned profits." He smiles.

I smile too.

There is a soft knock on the door. It opens, and Suzanne enters. Maybe she's here to explain this pesky noise. It'll be a relief finally to get to the bottom of it, find out they're polishing the floor in the hall, something like that. But Suzanne, with what looks like a memo in her hand, doesn't utter a word. She leans in and shows the memo to Jack. They huddle together over Jack's desk, studying it. After a minute, Jack nods. Suzanne withdraws, closing the door behind her.

Jack stands and moves to the window. Hands in his pockets, he strikes an almost philosophical pose. "The thing of it is, Michael," he says, "from a strategic standpoint, security provides no tangible rewards to subscribers." He smiles grimly out at the fog. "Until there are losses, unfortunately, the client may well drift into the belief that the time and energy invested in security have been wasted."

My eyes fall on that book on Jack's desk. It looks familiar. I'm squinting at the words crowded along the spine, lettered in black capitals—-*POST POSTMODERN: PAINTING, SCULPTURE, MIXED MEDIA, AND BEYOND.*

Leaning forward, I can clearly see a bookmark, perhaps some two-thirds of the way into the book. Of course, there is no way of knowing the exact page. On the edge of the sofa, I'm imagining reaching for the book. I'm actually on the verge of doing it when Jack spins around to face me.

"Penetration, Michael," he says. "Penetration. We can't afford to remain reactive. We want to be at least one step ahead. Both for our own good, and for the customer's good. Are you following me here?"

"So . . . you think Vince is a bit too reactive?"

"You've noticed too then?"

"Well, I would have said *cautious*."

Jack chuckles. Returning to his desk, he lowers himself into his chair. "And what good would caution do for the employees of ZACTRON?"

Of course, I can't answer that one.

Jack seems to have forgotten about the book. Instead he reaches across his desk and, with one finger, pulls that sheet of paper to where he can stare at it. When you come right down to it, he is an ugly son of a gun, Jack. The Adam's apple and those ears. And his mouth, as if the skin has been rubbed raw. "Human beings, Michael," that mouth says, "they're the weakest link in the security regimen of any system."

Jack might have a point there. Then again, sitting here in this office of his, I'm having trouble keeping track of so many things at once. My styrofoam cup weighs too much. Glancing into it, I see it's essentially full. What I'd really like to do is gather my thoughts—such as they are—brace myself for the final onslaught: Jack's concluding question.

But it never comes. At some point, Jack abruptly leans back in his swivel chair, crosses his legs, and thanks me for my candor. There is, as far as I can tell, no hint of ill will.

On the way out, I take a peek at that sheet of paper on his desk. It appears to be some kind of list. At the top is the heading, OVERARCHING OBJECTIVES.

With errands to run, I leave work a couple of minutes early. Outside, the fog is so thick, just walking those few yards across the parking lot, I feel the damp already in my clothes. I'm bending, opening my car door when I hear something familiar, a certain rhythmic squeaking. I look over toward the flower beds in front of Argus Towers, where the sound is coming from, and, sure enough, there among the hedges is Swenson! He's pushing his wheelbarrow heaped with some reddish brown stuff, probably bark mulch. Then I realize, no, he isn't Swenson. Though he certainly bears a strong resemblance to him, especially in the fog. And at that moment, the guy actually looks over and returns my stare, as if he senses me watching him. No, this is definitely not Swenson. This guy, whoever he is, I don't like the looks of.

On the drive home, I'm wrestling with my feelings about the meeting with Jack. On the one hand I'm relieved, really, that Stan and I aren't on the hit list. But Vince! What has that poor guy ever done but work like a slave? I mean, here's someone who has given everything to the company. Though that might be exactly Jack's point. That unquestioning devotion, that lifelong dedication—it could make a man too deliberate, not quick enough on his feet. As Jack put it, too reactive. That could, I suppose, prove a liability.

The Woods

HERE WE ARE for the first time, peering around among the tree trunks. He has said so little about this place. We have come out of naked curiosity. It is cool and quiet in here, in some peculiar way making everything look tall. We don't pause for very long. In these woods one wants to keep moving. This may be counterintuitive. But standing still here, one has the impression, that would be the way to lose oneself.

Still, we are taking our time. We don't want to miss anything.

The woods appear old beyond reckoning. That bird calling just now in the distance seems more a remembrance than an actual sound. Here under this canopy of green the air hangs like damp smoke. Whatever light flutters in from above seems not to know what to do with itself and is quickly lost. We thread our way among ferns that brush against our shoulders. Thick roots snake along the ground. There is no denying a certain presence here, a trace of something unfinished, perhaps, from long ago.

The bird calls a second time. We stop and listen. And now something else—here in the complicating hush of this understory, we're aware of an almost musical sound, which at first we mistook for silence. We can see it just ahead: the brook tumbling disconcertingly down the broken, sloping floor of the forest. The purl and gurgle and splash of this restless ribbon of water continues as far in either direction as we can be assumed to hear through the confusion of rocks and tree trunks and foliage. One can tell just from looking at it, the brook never stops running. Even in drier months it is somehow supplied with water.

It appears other people have walked in these woods before us. There is a path. And at the place where it crosses the brook, a primitive footbridge has been fashioned out of logs and planks. Though sturdily made, the footbridge has darkened and weathered with age. In the failing light of dusk, its outline blends until it seems almost to have grown into place, a part of the enveloping forest.

The brook, the path, the footbridge. Sitting upstairs at his desk in his study not a quarter mile from here, he knows nothing about any of this. He would be surprised to find out. We, however, have been making our way carefully in the other direction, away from him, through these woods. Looking around, we can't see an end to them.

F OR THE MOMENT, I've stopped reading. Not that I've run out of poems. Nowhere near it. But—who knows?—I thought I'd give it a shot. Well, not really, but just to see what might happen . . . if I tried to write one myself. A poem, that is.

I don't mean it in that way. Not an actual poem, in other words, but just to play around a little. I'm here at my desk, near dusk. I've been sitting this way for awhile. "Desk Near Dusk," that could be a title. Or not. It's just one of the decisions a poet would have to make. One of the many. So, I have to ask, is this how it's done?—all this waiting? My pencil, its point needle-sharp, is poised over the clean paper. I'm sitting, my gaze dead-center on that window, expectantly, it seems.

I used to be wilder. I used to have thoughts. All kinds of thoughts, who knows where they were leading me? I'd wonder about things: the Ice Ages, for example. Or about living in a hut, somewhere up on the tundra. But what happened was, Brenda came along. Brenda put an end to all that, scorched it right out of me. I had to forget about it. I thought I was walking away cleansed. The tundra, I never found out about that. That's the sad part.

Close to quitting time, I'm putting my office in order when I hear a gasp from Sonya. I look, and there in the outer office Stan has appeared, solemnly presenting some kind of sword in a sheath.

"What the hell?" I say.

"The machete," he says. He draws the blade and thrusts it at the air as if, by way of demonstration, he might be aiming to do away with the ceiling tiles.

The blade glints in the fluorescent light.

"Where did you get that?"

"Little gun shop in Tijuana." He is gazing at the machete as if with fatherly pride. "This particular weapon took part in the Mexican Revolution."

Sonya can't take her eyes off it. "My God," she says.

Stan grins. "This baby could tell some stories."

Sonya says, "I don't think I want to hear them."

From where I'm standing, the blade looks awfully sharp. "Jesus, Stan," I say. "I can't use that on weeds."

"Why the hell not? That's exactly what it was designed for. The tougher the weeds the better. It'll give you a nice margin of safety, in terms of a firebreak."

Sonya nods. This makes perfect sense to her.

"Firebreak." I say.

Stan sheathes the machete in the leather scabbard, which is impressively decorated with metal work and gems and braided leather fringe. He looks pretty good handling it, as though he's practiced.

Sonya makes a face. "It's scary."

Stan hands the machete over to me. "Here you go, Michael. Take no prisoners."

I accept the machete from him with both hands, holding it horizontally. "Well," I say. "I'll certainly take good care of this."

Stan winks at Sonya, then turns and leaves.

Even after he's gone, I'm still holding the machete in that same way, as if it were some sort of sacrificial weapon.

Sonya pouts her lower lip out, blows some stray hair out of her face. "Are you really going to use it to cut weeds?" she says.

I can't think of what to say.

Sonya looks at me funny, and I realize I've been staring at her. I don't know how not to. Sonya, for all practical purposes, the eighth wonder of the world.

"Yeah," I say, "maybe I will."

Needing someplace else to put my eyes, I unsheathe the blade for a closer look. Testing it against my thumb, I actually draw blood. I'm wondering. Maybe it could be useful against snakes.

On my way home, the machete attracts quite a few stares. I'm carrying it at my side, matter-of-factly, trying not to make a big deal of it. But as I'm crossing the lobby, some guys from accounting are pouring out of an elevator. "Whoa, Lancelot," Phil Morrow shouts, "heading out to slay some dragons?" And then there's Vince Marconi, the last person I want to bump into. He catches sight of me in the parking lot. Frozen in the act of ducking into his car, he looks as though he can't believe his eyes. "What the blazes, Benson!" That's all he says.

Too late now, but it would have been better, of course, to wrap the thing in a black plastic bag.

I AM ENTERING the house through the garage when I see my golf bag leaning against the outer wall—where I would never put it. Leaving the door ajar, I approach the bag carefully, alert for any movement, anything else that might be out of place. My senses feel bright, perfectly tuned. Enough of this monkey business. I am surprised, actually, how much it upsets me. I'm standing over the bag, my teeth grinding away, my breath laboring, as if I'm about to give birth to something.

Taking inventory, I see that the four-iron is missing. The goddamned four-iron!

I search the garage, the front and back yards—the club is gone. Pure and simple. I look up into the sky—or what would be the sky, if it weren't for this endlessly churning fog—exasperation and helplessness flooding over me like a tide. The thing is I don't even care about my damned golf clubs. But these security breaches, these intrusions into my life I will not stand for.

I'm all the way upstairs in the bedroom, changing—practically naked—when, looking out the window, I spot the iron propped against a tree at the edge of the woods.

I'm staring at it all the time I'm dressing. I don't quite trust the sight of it there, as though, if I would take my eyes away for an instant, it might disappear. I lace up my shoes, then head downstairs and out the back door. Right away my eyes locate the iron still leaning against the tree. Letting the screen door close carefully, I pause there on the landing, surveying the yard, the line of trees along the edge of the woods. I don't see anything out of the ordinary, although somehow things seem awfully quiet.

Brenda, I know, is still at her painting class. Or should be. Neither Swenson nor his truck is anywhere to be seen.

I take the porch steps slowly, noiselessly, playing at this cat-and-mouse game—that's the way it feels. I start across the yard. The woods look at first so familiar, I almost can't see them. But the closer I get, the more it seems something isn't right. It's as if I'm watching a movie of the woods with the sound turned off.

I stop. I'm about five or six feet from the club. The air here seems cooler, and maybe—though it sounds strange to say—not so friendly. I'm not used to seeing the woods from this angle. Up this close, it's a little like being inside them.

I reach and grab ahold of the iron. The handle is damp, cold. Apparently it's been there for awhile, leaning against the tree. I whip the club back and forth. The action seems all right. I sight along the shaft and then along the blade. I examine the head from different angles, slide my thumb into the cavity back, where it fits nicely, the way it always does. It feels good, in fact, to have the club in my hand again. As far as I can tell, there isn't a thing wrong with it. It might as well have climbed out of the bag and walked here to the edge of the yard on its own.

But hold it now! I hear something. So close by and sudden, it throws a shiver right through me. I freeze, listening, every muscle taut. It's coming from in the woods—a woman's voice. And then it hits me. Who else could it be?

Before I even give it a thought, I'm bounding in among the trees. Branches from the underbrush are snapping me in the face. I feel confused, actually clumsy at first. But, a short distance in, I'm surprised to see there's a trail. I follow it.

After a minute I stop to catch my breath. It may be I've been making too much noise. I wouldn't want to lose the advantage of surprise. Imagining what sort of person might be out in an area like this, I have to say, it gives me pause. Looking back, I can no longer see any sign of the yard. I wonder just how far I've come. The woods are awfully gloomy, and a bit disorienting. There is something about the place that makes me very uneasy. I'm surrounded completely by trees. Not only straight, vertical, healthy trees, as you might expect, but also dead trees, fallen and leaning, vines creeping up and around them. Huge trunks, maybe hundreds of years old, must have at some point come crashing down. As big around as cars, they lie now on the forest floor, covered with moss. Other trunks have grown twisted or sideways or have been broken off by the fall of larger trees. It's a kind of chaos, really. This Swenson calls himself a forester. I wonder why he and his crew haven't been in here to clean some of this up. At least make an effort.

I hear the voice again—really close this time, just over the next little rise. And, now that my breathing has calmed, I hear something else—like an increase in wind. Except that there is no wind in here. The air is utterly still. I begin again silently, walking cautiously now, placing my feet the way I imagine a woodsman or a hunter might. I crest the next little slope, and, lo and behold, there she is, sitting on a rock, talking to a dog. The dog is standing squarely in a brook. Which is the other sound I heard.

Quiet as I am, she senses me somehow right away. And then I see how. Her dog is staring straight at me.

The woman seems young—a girl, really, though there is something (I can't quite tell what) odd about her face. And just as last time, she is dressed all in gray: not in a robe as I thought, but pants and a kind of shawl she's wrapped around herself.

She springs immediately to her feet on the rock, looking not so much afraid as maybe a bit defiant.

I take a step toward her, but the dog makes me think twice.

She grins. "What happened? You lose your ball?"

Glancing down, I am embarrassed to find the four-iron still in my hand.

"Listen," I say. I like the level, measured tone of my voice, making it clear that I'm not fooling around, that I mean business. "If you're the one who's been messing with my clubs . . . "

But her grin breaks wide open. She essentially laughs in my face. Not a calculated sort of laugh, but giggly, out of control.

After all that I have been through lately, not to mention tracking her down out here in this wilderness, I find her reaction infuriating. My voice is losing a bit of its restraint when I say, "So you think this is funny." I take a step closer.

She makes a clicking sound to the dog, and the two of them bolt.

Dog or no dog, I take off right after her.

But she's surprisingly quick, and I'm soon losing ground. I have to stop. With the last of my breath and all the authority I can summon, I yell, "I'm warning you, God-damn it! Whoever you are, you stay the hell out of my yard!"

Far in the distance, I hear her crazy laughter. It's eerie, careening among the branches overhead.

I'd like to catch the girl and shake some sense into her. I'm actually screaming now, "You'd better believe it, you nut case!" In a rage, I swing the club in her direction, accidentally clipping a couple of ferns at the base. Almost as tall as I am, they collapse like feathers to the ground, where they lie together as if taken by surprise.

I'm so worked up, so angry, it takes me a minute to understand that maybe screaming wasn't the smartest course of action. How do I know, after all, that the girl doesn't have allies?—tattooed hoodlums draped in animal skins, packing knives and pellet guns.

The little brook bubbles beside the trail—the only sound in this ringing silence. I notice a greenish cast to the air, as if this air has never been anywhere else but in a forest. My mind seems to slow down. I'm not used to thinking around trees so large, so ancient. On every side of me, the woods seem endless. I don't know where I am exactly or just how far from the yard I've ventured.

I pause only a moment before starting back along the path. But in that moment, I feel something. I'm not sure I can describe it. It is as though everything—every tree and fern and rock—has turned a little toward me, the way flowers will turn toward the light. Walking, I'm trying to think about life in the house. I've got to put this club away, and there is dinner to prepare. I get a pretty good pace going.

ZACTRON HAS YET AGAIN been violated. Wendell Carlson stopped by personally to advise me that he was, in effect, disappointed. He got his point across all right. I tried putting it a little more in context, as a part of the general trend these days. "When it rains, it pours," I said. Wendell was in no mood to be philosophical.

Stan and I are working on it, as usual, in my office. "To chase ghosts, you need to be a ghost." Stan punctuates with a sip of coffee. "Never operate out of your own office." By which of course he means his. Which suits me well enough. Stan's office is a dingy ground-level hovel with cement-block walls and a window looking out on a lot of pipes. He doesn't mind. As a matter of fact, he requested that room. Management, he claims, can't spy on him so easily down there.

Anyway here he is again at my machine. I'm sitting on the table behind him and looking over his shoulder.

The black hat meanwhile, far from idle, has been inventing fresh configurations of headache for us, nearly tripling the number of employees he's stolen. And he has altered his signature. This time, when we rearrange the first letters of last names, we get nothing.

"It's a never-ending battle," Stan says. Then he adds, in that wistful, faraway voice of his, "And over all too quick. All too quick."

"That's a contradiction."

"Life is a contradiction," he says.

I'm about to accuse him of shifting his ground. But I let it drop. Instead I ask, "So where do we go from here?"

"I don't know." Stan leans back, folds his arms. He sits quiet for a minute. "Say we fabricate a honeypot. Use my server downstairs as the decoy. Give us a chance to observe the son of a bitch in action."

"I like it."

"As for this mess . . . ." He shakes his head.

Lunch time rolls around, and we send out for sandwiches. We're trying one thing and, a few minutes later, another thing. We're not making headway. My office smells like a delicatessen, and there's something else that doesn't feel quite right. I get up to open the window a crack, then decide against it.

Waiting for a sequence of data to unpack, Stan lets his eyes fall on the volume of Pablo Neruda's *Selected Poems* at the corner of the table. He picks it up, studies the front cover, then the back. He gives me a look that's hard to decipher.

"He's really good," I say.

"I know that. But I didn't know *you* did." He opens the book to where I've left the bookmark.

"I'm a man of surprises," I say.

Stan stares at the page. Then his voice startles me. It's Stan's voice all right, the same one, but suddenly beautiful somehow. He's reading:

> They move in the fullness of time
> from the once-fragrant houses
> and the char of the twilight.
>
> They see and do not see the waters,
> they write signs with their walking sticks,
> and the sea blots their signatures.
>
> Then the ancients move off
> on frail bird's feet, upraised,
> while a runaway surf
> travels naked in the wind.

Stan's voice trails off a little near the end, a bit uneven, and his expression flickers in a way I've never seen before. I keep watching him. It's as if some tiny trace of a new kind of order might be finding its way into the world.

"That was nice," I say.

He shuts the book. He doesn't say anything.

Then a moment later, without warning, he rises and moves to the window. He stares out at the fog, or maybe at something he's imagining beyond the fog. He says, "Don't tell anyone." There's a long silence before he adds, "I've been thinking of buying a boat."

I don't want to lose this moment. It's what I was talking about. I'd like to hold everything just as it is. So I'm still listening. But what I hear is Sonya's voice in the outer office. Through the crack of the open door, I catch a glimpse of Vince standing in front of Sonya's desk. Vince looks terrible. I go to the door, but by the time I get there he has already left.

Sonya shrugs. "That was Vince. He says he'll come back."

"Is he all right?"

"He says he has a bug."

"That's what he came to tell me?"

"I don't think so."

From where I'm standing I have a full, high-definition view of Sonya's legs. But even that isn't enough to hold me. I shut the door quickly, as if there might still be something of Vince out there, something not so nice, wanting to get in. Just as easily as that, the feeling is back, that gnawing dread. Stan's boat, his beautiful voice—they've disappeared somewhere, like dissolved pieces of some dream.

Cleaning up the trash from lunch, I get the idea to try middle initials.

Stan crumples his sandwich wrapper into a ball and lets fly at my trash can. It goes in. "Why not," he says.

It takes ten minutes of rearranging before we come up with a communication. It says, "Forget about chains. Try welding the lids onto the cans."

Stan stares. "What's that supposed to mean?"

In the car on the way home, I have more than enough to think about. But whatever is going on in my head, I wouldn't call it thinking. Who knows how fast I'm driving. I look at the speedometer: the numbers are meaningless. The entire landscape is a blur—I don't know what to make of it. I need to recognize something in a hurry.

I pull over to the side of the road, traffic whizzing past. The pavement is wet, that much is obvious. Every ten seconds or so, the wipers make a pass, clearing the windshield of mist. This happens over and over—how many times, I can't keep track. But it is something I can count on. I look around for others.

The car doors are locked. The engine is running. I'm sitting behind the wheel, my limbs entirely slack, as if the feeling has gone out of them, which it hasn't. My posture, I believe, is excellent. My eyes stray to the glove compartment. I'm not going to open it. I'm not even going to think about opening it. There are probably a dozen things I could do at this point, but I can't bring myself to contemplate a single one.

After awhile something inside me clicks, I don't know what. I put the car in gear, pull out into the flow of traffic, other car horns blaring. I like the sound, it's one I've heard before. Coming up to lane speed, I glance at myself in the rearview mirror, and it's true, I have a grin on my face. I don't know why. Maybe it's the excitement—there is that to be said for it.

Turning into the driveway is like waking up. Especially now that I have to wait for a car leaving. A silver-gray Camry, of course. Ted's car. As he pulls out onto Forest Drive, Ted waves and smiles broadly. I'm getting to know that smile pretty well.

I enter the kitchen through the garage, and there is Brenda standing by the telephone—a paintbrush in her hand.

When I glare at her, she looks at me blankly.

The silence weighs.

"All right," she says finally. "What's the problem?"

I pretend at first that I don't know what she means. Then I make a point of seeing the paintbrush. "You and Ted have been painting up a storm, have you?"

"What are you talking about?"

I shake my head. In full view of her, I toss my jacket on the kitchen counter, something I never do. I don't know what I'm waiting for. For weeks now I've been dying to let her know. I suppose no moment can ever be sufficient to the occasion.

She's staring at me—I can feel it.

I open the fridge, grab a Corona, pop the cap off. In the process, the cap drops through my fingers and dances across the floor tile. I watch it with interest, the way I might watch an exceptionally fine putt. I raise the bottle and suck down a good swig of beer.

These also are things I never do.

Brenda folds her arms, and waits, the paintbrush jutting from between her fingers like some cigarette holder. Greta Garbo couldn't have done it better. And I'm thinking, *this*. *This* I'm losing to that dilettante? That real estate salesman?

She says, "For God's sake what is it?"

I take another swig of Corona, turn and stare out the kitchen window at the back lawn. That soft expanse of green—it has a calming effect. My voice is satisfyingly vacant when I say, "I'm really sick of Ted hanging around here." It feels right. I'm not talking to her. I'm simply sharing my opinions with the lawn.

She laughs. "Why?"

"You figure it out." Looking her right in the eye, I raise the Corona again to my lips. I swear, the stuff has never tasted better. With one finger, I push open the screen door, and all at once I'm outside.

It is something like exhilaration propelling me down the steps and lightly over the grass. For the next half hour, I am preoccupied reacquainting myself with our many flowers and shrubs. My hand wrapped around the neck of the beer bottle as if it were some botanist's tool, I meander about the yard, stopping to inspect a hollyhock here, a juniper there. Nothing is beneath my interest. All of it is surprising and mildly wonderful. At one point I look up, for it even seems that the fog might be lifting. But no. No, it's just a temporary brightening.

Inevitably, however, there is dinner. Just the two of us sitting across that table from one another. Brenda keeps eyeing me.

She plucks an olive out of the dish, twists her glass of pinot by the stem, and smiles playfully. "You know," she says, "he's been asking about you."

I stare at her.

"Actually . . . I'm not supposed to tell you this, Michael. But he is quite taken with you." There is an unfamiliar tone to her voice, girlish, almost giggly. I wonder if she's had too much wine.

"Who are you talking about?"

"Ted, of course. You were the one who brought him up."

Equanimity, at moments like this, doesn't come easily. I nod. "Oh, right. I see. I'm the apple of Ted's eye, is that it? That's very interesting."

"It's true. He's gay." She winks. "He thinks you're the bee's knees."

"Right." Though my own wine glass isn't quite empty, I reach for the bottle. "You expect me to believe that."

"You can believe what you want. But I'm warning you, Michael, the next time you pass him on the front walk, don't be surprised if he grabs you."

Feeling her toes graze my leg, I pull my leg away. "Cut the crap, Brenda."

I fill my glass, set the bottle down. There, right in front of me, is the remainder of my dinner. It isn't complicated, what I need to do. First off, I pick up my glass. At least there is the reassuring taste of the wine. I employ my fork, cutting and spearing carrot disks, nuggets of crab cake. I mop up dressing with what's left of my salad. I sip more wine.

Inside, needless to say, I'm not as composed as I pretend. I'm considering how to respond, or whether to respond at all. I set the wine glass down, pick it up again. I chuckle, shake my head.

Brenda tilts her gaze at me.

"I'll tell you something, Brenda. I don't know who you are anymore." This is what I imagine myself saying. But I'm looking for exactly the right moment, and the words never quite come out. Other retorts loom, then slip away. None of them seems to score a direct hit. At some point it is clear from Brenda's expression that she has left the conversation behind. Why should I be dredging it up? I finish my dinner in what I hope passes for righteous silence.

When Brenda finally stands and leaves the table, I don't budge. I'm in no hurry. Studying the wine at the bottom of my glass, I am for some reason reminded of the girl in gray. That wild creature roaming the woods with her dog. Quite possibly a little loony. I wonder whether she knows what a computer is. I wonder whether she's dangerous.

I try to imagine, at this precise moment, where she is.

Before bed I pause in front of the bathroom mirror, taking stock of things. I'm standing in my underwear, as if at attention. The lights on either side of the mirror appear unnaturally bright, as of course they should. The tile gleams. I can see every detail in front of me, every sparkle and blemish on the faucets. Not two feet away, my toothbrush is hanging from the rack over the sink. I've seen it there before. Still, I give it a long, hard stare.

Behind me in the dark of the bedroom, Brenda makes some slight noise, clearing her throat perhaps.

In the mirror, reflected, I can see myself looking back.

It's me. I'm almost positive.

I OPEN my eyes and know immediately where I am. I look around. Everything in the bedroom is still there, Brenda next to me, sound asleep. Nothing has changed. The first cold glimmer of daylight is leaking already in through the windows. It gives me an uneasy feeling. I don't waste time getting out of bed. Whatever is going to happen, I want to be on my feet.

Showering, dressing, pouring a glass of orange juice, venturing out the front door, maneuvering down the driveway—over and over I'm thinking, this could be the last time I do this.

But then, at work, nothing. The morning slides by indifferently, except that, if I'm not mistaken, everyone seems a little nervous. I can't get eye contact.

I go looking for Stan. I find him hunched over his desk, making adjustments to his server. His office is like a tunnel, with obstacles. Trying to squeeze past him to where I can see what he's doing, I bump my head on an I-beam. For awhile neither of us says anything. Now and then he takes a swig from what looks like cold coffee, which sits on the corner of his desk next to half a cruller. I just stand there. But I'm watching him closely.

Stan says, "You ever notice how they call the place Argus Towers and there's only one tower?"

I nod. It's true, I have noticed.

I look around at the obstructions looming near my head—beams, pipes, wiring, light fixtures, the sort of stuff that in a normal office would be hidden by ceiling tiles. Here it's right at eye level. There's no getting away from it. On the tiny window of his office, beads of fog are accumulating, leaking over the glass, blurring the tangle of pipes outside into a slithery sort of liquidity.

Stan reaches, exchanges one Phillips screwdriver for another. "Anyway," he says, "it's not even a tower, it's just a lousy tall building."

I'm not about to argue with him. I'm happy enough just to hear his voice, a voice that seems actually directed at me. I stand with my hands in my pockets, enjoying this meeting of the minds.

I'm supposed to have a ten o'clock with Mel Pettigrew, but he doesn't show up. Nobody's seen him. Sonya calls his house and leaves a message. I ask her to keep a lookout for Mel. Scratching something on a note pad, she nods but doesn't look up.

I enter my office, close the door. Leaning against it, I survey the room—the table, the window, the filing cabinet, the desk. What else? Any more eye openers? It's a waiting game.

I'm in the car on the way home, half-listening to the news, when I hear mention of someone familiar: Melvin Pettigrew. The sound of that name, delivered by the voice of the newscaster, has a certain startling shape to it. But it's there and gone before I understand anything of what is said. For the second time in as many days, I veer over into the breakdown lane and up onto the grass. I don't know why I do this. Mel Pettigrew is nothing to me. And, anyway, I have no idea what he's involved in. It's just a feeling.

Traffic, just like the last time, continues zipping by as if nothing at all has happened. As if nothing could ever happen outside the orbits of these automobiles. As if everything, everything depended on this incessant velocity. I reach, shut the radio off. I'd like to hold everything still just for a moment. I'd like things to stop moving. Gusts from the passing trucks wrestle the car and flatten the roadside grass. The sparrows flitting and pecking the gravel seem used to this. Ignoring the trucks, they eye my car warily. In what's left of the drizzling light, the grass almost glows. An unbearably rich brown, rippling in the breeze, it hardly seems real.

I sit. I don't know where the time goes. Eventually the traffic subsides. Checking the dashboard clock, I realize I've been here close to an hour. Dusk is coming on fast, and it occurs to me for the first time that we may never be seeing the sun again, at least not the way we used to. All at once now the sparrows scatter as if sucked away by vacuum. I watch their individual bodies merge and sweep in flight, maybe fifteen or twenty of them, arcing out of sight into the mist over the trees. Quickly I put the car in gear and give it gas. Old Mel Pettigrew—I wonder what he could be up to that would merit attention on the news. Already I'm afraid for him.

What Else?

THE OFFICE, at this irretrievable hour of the night, is empty of people but not of things. Everything is exactly as he left it, there is no telling how long ago. The desk and chair, the bookcase, the filing cabinet. The carpet. Nothing has changed—except that all of it, we can't help noticing, seems a shade less familiar. What are these things, really? In the half-lit stillness of this doubtful hour, even ordinary pieces of furniture appear freakish, tumid, absurd, as if things left long enough idle might forfeit their purpose and eventually their substance. The scene could be mistaken for a photograph of an office, distorted by the trick of some lens, if it weren't for the occasional clicks and brightenings in the silence and, high among the tiles of the ceiling, the rush of air through a ventilation register.

Gray would want to prevail in this place. But the fog outside the window is glowing like a vapor on fire, likely from the lamps in the parking lot, tinting the room orange. The night feels well advanced, perhaps even close to morning. We could imagine somewhere already a softening in the eastern sky, the horizon pulling itself together. But not here, not outside this window, where there is no view of anything except for that lurid mist urging itself against the glass.

And now another consideration—there are voices in the building. Men's voices. Muted, monotonous, they percolate as if through the floor, as if through time. The sound of their talk produces here in this room an even more dire stillness, as though the dustless and hard-angled office were dreading just such a complication. Somewhere a file drawer slowly closes with a rumble and thud that sound like distant thunder. The talk falls silent, then resumes—an incoherent litany of not-quite words. Perhaps several times in the midst of this the name Michael arises. Then again, perhaps it doesn't. We can't be certain.

AS SOON AS I turn onto Forest Drive, I see the flashing blue lights of an approaching police cruiser. I slow down, an instinctive reaction, though I am probably under the limit to begin with. The cruiser is crawling along, its window rolled down. The officer at the wheel swivels his head toward me as we pass. I wave, but he doesn't wave back. Through the woods ahead I see more blue lights and, when the road bends left, another police car. This officer, talking on his radio, looks me over too.

At the corner of Glen a third patrol car is waiting perpendicular to Forest with only its parking lights on. Sure enough, as soon as I pass, it pulls out behind me, lights flashing. The siren yips, just once—an added pinprick of humiliation. I pull over. There is the usual exchange of documents: license, registration, proof of insurance. He sorts through all of this.

"Michael Benson." The way he says it, I'm not sure if it's a statement or a question.

"That's right," I say. "I live about a block from here." I point in the direction of our house, but he's not looking. There's a strain in my voice that I don't like the sound of.

"Do you?" he says, his voice flat. And for the first time today, I get eye contact.

He disappears. In my side-view mirror I see him walk back to his cruiser and duck inside with my documents. He's in there for a long time, his blue lights pulsing, casting their aura of shame. Other cars pass, their occupants free to travel the road.

When he finally returns, he says, "I'm going to ask you to step out of your vehicle."

I hesitate. "I'm sorry, is there something wrong?"

"Please, step out of your vehicle, if you would, sir."

I undo my seat belt, open the door, and step out onto the fresh, practically unblemished asphalt of Forest Drive. It seems the wrong surface to support a miscarriage of justice.

The officer's left hand is aiming a flashlight at me. And, if I'm not mistaken, his right hand is not far away from his gun.

He says, "Place your hands on the roof of your vehicle. Feet apart please."

"Wait, I don't understand . . . ."

"Hands on the roof of your vehicle, sir, if you would."

I do as he asks. And in that moment, as soon as my hands touch the cold of the metal roof, I am aware of something different, a new taste, dry and bitter at the back of my mouth. I understand that I have crossed a boundary. I have stepped over to the other side of things now, the darker side. The side of the lost, the irreclaimable. I can feel the pull in that direction. It wouldn't take much, it seems. One little nudge could break you loose. You'd never find your way back.

While he's frisking me, another police cruiser, approaching from ahead, slows. It crosses the road and parks, its headlights to my headlights. They have me boxed in.

This new officer emerges, glances at the first with a little flip of his eyebrows.

The first officer says, "Five-fourteen, Tom." Finished frisking, he has me step away from the car.

Officer Tom walks around the passenger side of my car, probing through the windows with his flashlight. He opens the back door and reaches in, and my heart sinks. I see him pull out the machete. He studies it. I don't like the look on his face when he hands it over the hood.

The first officer takes it. "What's this?" he says.

"It's a machete," I say. "I'm borrowing it. I need to get rid of some weeds."

"Weeds," the first officer says.

"Yeah. In our back yard."

The two officers exchange glances.

"Pretty aggressive, are they?" the first one says.

Tom has the front passenger door open now, and he's rummaging around the seat. When he straightens, he has one of my books in his hand. He squints at the cover, then opens it, flips through a couple of pages.

"Chinese poetry," I say. "T'ang Dynasty."

The two look at one another.

"Tang, huh?" Tom says. He keeps flipping the pages.

The first officer sets the machete aside on the hood of my car. "Mr. Benson," he says. "Were you aware that the registration has lapsed on your Legacy?"

"Pardon?"

"Dark green 98 wagon." He pauses, refers to a pad. "Vehicle number JHQ41109753."

"We don't own that car anymore."

Turning his attention and his flashlight back to the car interior, he seems to have lost interest in his own question, not to mention my answer. "Is that right?" he says.

Tom has come around to join us now. He's examining the blade of the machete. He rubs his thumb across it, then looks at me.

"It's pretty sharp," I say.

Tom lifts his eyebrows. He holds the machete blade in the headlights, squinting. I hear him mumble to the first officer, "Does that look like blood on there?"

The first one leans in. They study the blade together in silence.

They sit me down in the back of the second cruiser while the first officer puts through calls on his radio. They pop my trunk open, root around in there, although there's nothing in it. Now and then they ask me another question.

After about forty-five minutes they let me go. They give me back the book. The first officer hands me the machete. His eyes are cold, empty-looking. When I move to take it, he pulls it back just out of my reach. Then he gives it to me.

"You be careful with that," Tom says. "Chinese poetry. In the wrong hands, it could be dangerous."

The first officer is studying me closely. He doesn't smile.

Entering the house through the garage, I can hear Brenda on the phone. When I open the kitchen door, she looks up, delivers a withering glare. Holding her hand over the mouthpiece, she says, "Where have you been?"

"I got stopped by the police. What's going on? It's like a war zone out there."

But she's back listening to whoever is on the line. Sybil would be my guess.

I turn and head down the hall. Halfway up the stairs I hear her voice calling after me, "You could have phoned."

I pause. I have a hand on the railing, one foot on one step, one foot on another. What is this? Brenda, the adulteress, concerned about the safety of her husband? I'm racking my brains for a suitable response, but it's no use. For the rest of the way up the stairs, it's two steps at a time.

Changing my clothes, I'm continually glancing out the bedroom window. There is no daylight left out there, but the backyard floodlights are switched on. I keep an eye on the grass. It looks peaceful, the lawn at night. Entering the study, still buttoning my shirt, I notice my hands are shaking. I'm not sure where to begin. I believe what I need more than anything right now is a moment to stop and think. I'm standing, contemplating the stack of books on my desk, when the doorway darkens, and I turn to see Brenda. She's leaning against the jamb, her arms folded as if she's hugging herself.

"I don't know if you've heard," she says.

"About what?"

"Mel." Her voice fades to the point where I'm leaning forward to hear her. "They found him this morning, stretched out on his patio."

"There was something on the news. But he's dead? Mel?"

"They said it looked like a heart attack." She steps into the room and sits on the ship's locker by the desk. "The funny thing—Janet said she was outside earlier filling her bird feeder. She said she thought she heard him yell."

"So . . . what are you saying?"

"I don't know," she says. "I don't know."

"Jesus."

I hear a noise, and now I notice lights and movement outside. I go to the window in time to see a Brandewoode security squad, complete with German shepherds, working their way over our lawn. Three guys suited up in black, carrying rifles and phones and, it looks like, GPS equipment.

I say, "It's just a heart attack, right? I don't understand why the police are involved."

"Well, evidently something has made them suspicious."

Around the edge of the woods, the dogs get interested. They strain at their leashes, nosing among the rhododendrons.

"A heart attack," I say. I'm shaking my head.

Brenda says, "This is the third or fourth time they've been through here today. Something seems to be driving the dogs crazy."

"Maybe that person, whoever it is, that's been after our trash."

She looks at me blankly, then turns vaguely toward the window. Her expression, I can see, has undergone a change. As if, ten seconds ago, there may have been a smile there. But there isn't one now. It's impossible to tell what's going on inside that head of hers. After all, there she is, what's left of my Brenda. And even now after all that's happened, with a twinge of longing, I am struck with the truth of it—she is far and away the most beautiful woman I've ever known.

She says, "Sybil packed up this morning. She booked a flight to Belize."

I couldn't care less about Sybil. I'm hit with a sudden surge of emotion. "Brenda," I say after a minute, "I just want you to know that . . . whatever happens, I've enjoyed these years we've been together."

She looks at me then, really looks at me. I can feel the depth of her gaze. She seems to be considering her words carefully. Finally she says, "You know, you could really use a haircut, Michael."

I'M THINKING something is not quite square at Argus: "The Towers," as the employees like to call it (poor Mel Pettigrew, for example). Something is not quite plumb. There seems to be all the usual activity out front. People look busy enough. But it feels more like a façade, as if the only real work is going on somewhere behind the scenes.

For me, the days here have taken on the consistency of glue. Not that there isn't work enough. The jobs have been queuing up. Likewise the e-mail. There are plenty of people running around, but never the person you want. I stop in to see Vince, and he just stepped out. I try Wendell Carlson. His door is locked—his secretary is nowhere to be found. I call several customers, all I get is voice mail.

And people's faces . . . there's something. I don't even want to think about it.

At some point I retreat into the men's room, where the flush on one of the urinals is stuck, manufacturing a continual rush of white noise. I push open the door to one of the stalls, enter and lock it and sit down on the toilet. I just sit there with my head between my knees, letting the sound of that flush wash over me. I don't know how long I'm in there. I don't hear anyone else come in. Maybe I even doze a little.

When I open my eyes, I have the feeling something has happened—I couldn't say what. I get up and open the stall door, poke my head out. The men's room is empty. I wash my hands and face, dry them with a towel, and, as nonchalantly as I can, head out into the hall.

There is no one in the hall. Rose, the receptionist in Customer Service, is not at her desk. I look in on Customer Service proper, a suite of four offices, with two additional secretaries. The place is deserted. Likewise, at the other end of the hall, Quality Assurance. Outside my office Sonya has disappeared. The entire seventh floor, as far as I can see, is empty.

I head for the elevator, then change my mind. I take the back stairs. On Level Six I open the door and lean out into the hall. Nothing but silence. Two floors down, on Level Four, the same thing. I just keep going.

On the ground floor I fling the door open, and there outside is the parking lot, just as it should be—full of cars. No people, just cars. I head straight for mine. I have no idea what I'm going to do, but the thought of my own car in the spot where I parked it this morning is irresistible. I could put the key in the ignition. There is at least a possibility that it would start. I could drive somewhere— where, I can figure out later.

I'm just about at the car when I hear sounds. And then I see them, out in front of Argus Towers, milling around in small groups by the shrubbery. Quality Assurance, Customer Service, Receiving, Ancillary Services—they're all there, gabbing and horsing around in the fog. And some of them, I see, beginning now to file back into the building.

Then I realize—a fire alarm. It must have gone off when I was in the men's room. I spot Sonya about the same time she sees me. I wave, but I don't stop, I don't change course. I continue straight to my car and open the door. I lean in and rummage around by the console. I need something in my hand, anything. Finally I pop the glove compartment and grab the owner's manual.

On the way home I stop at the hardware store. It's been somehow in the back of my mind to buy a bigger chain, one that can't be snapped like a clothesline. I ask for eight feet of the heaviest chain they carry. The links are thick, maybe too thick. I'm having second thoughts as I watch the salesman cut it. The handles of the bolt cutters must be four feet long. But it's done. I pick up three of the heaviest eyebolts I can find—the kind they use to secure anchors for telephone poles—and a couple of tubes of epoxy.

Holding onto the chain in the checkout line is making my arm sore. The thing must weight twenty pounds. The woman two customers ahead of me is counting out her change.

Before I know what's happening, I feel a hand clamp on my shoulder, and someone has me in an affectionate one-arm squeeze. I turn, and there—not six inches from my face—is Ted's eerily familiar grin. Of course, I jump. Luckily I don't drop the chain.

"Whoa, fella," Ted says.

"Jesus, you scared me," I say.

Ted laughs. "These are scary times."

"You can say that again," the cashier calls, though she's still ringing up the person ahead of me.

Ted leans in to me. "We have to stop meeting like this. Liquor store, hardware. Next it'll be the tanning salon."

I'm nodding, amusement—as I imagine it—written all over my face.

Ted's eyebrows arch when he notices the chain. "Wow, what have you got there? Little precaution for the hurricane?"

"No, no."

"That thing's big enough to moor your house with."

"No, we've had a problem with theft lately."

"Oh, right." Ted's face darkens with concern. "Brenda mentioned the trash."

"Yeah, and my golf clubs." The chain rattles as I set it on the counter. "What hurricane?"

"You haven't heard?"

"No. I've . . . had my mind on other things."

Ted's shopping basket, I see now, is full of flashlight batteries, drinking water, and duct tape. He's also picked out a hammer—even I can tell, the sort of hammer someone might buy who had never used a hammer before.

"Yeah," he says, "Category-Four. Supposed to arrive sometime the day after tomorrow."

"Hm!" I say.

The chain costs me $54.55. The cashier coaxes it along the counter into a double plastic bag. She doesn't lift it, but slides it and passes me the handles. "There," she says, animated. "Don't drop it on your foot."

"That's good advice," Ted says.

I nod. I can't think of a thing to say.

Ted can. He says, "Hey, listen, if you need any help battening things down, don't hesitate. Give me a buzz."

"Sure," I say. "I think we're all set."

He winks.

I find myself nodding goodbye to the two of them, Ted and the cashier standing there with twin smiles.

On my way out of the store, the chain is so heavy, I'm forced to gimp.

The chain lies in a lump behind my seat on the floor of the car. Over rough sections of road I hear it murmuring metallically inside its skin of plastic bag, reminding me that I'm not sure whether I want it there or not. It was barely fifteen minutes ago that I bought the thing without thoroughly rehearsing it through, and, the more I think about it, the less sense it makes. I should have thought of this before, of course. But suppose, for example, that I am stopped again by the police. Not that the chain is illegal—that's not what worries me. But, given my history, what plausible explanation could I come up with for possessing this monstrosity?—that it is part of a strategy to protect my trash?

I have to think of something fast. Traffic on the highway is fairly heavy. And now everyone squeezes right to make way for two state police cruisers flying past on the left, sirens wailing, lights flashing. They speed ahead, receding, fading, until all that remains of them are a flicker of blue pulses in the mist. Where they're headed, I don't want to know.

Suddenly on the left I spot that road I saw weeks ago running up into meadow. There's an opening in the oncoming lane. With no time to signal, I veer sharply. The guy behind me leans on his horn, but I make the turn all right.

I'm surprised, but also relieved at what I've just done. I have no idea where this detour will bring me. It's not that I aim to get rid of the chain. I'd just like more time to decide. The road climbs rapidly up through fog, winding along the boundary between autumn meadow and woods. It's impressive, the beauty of the scenery up here. No broad vistas. It's a close-up sort of beauty. A little like Brandewoode, only wilder. And I'd have to say, darker.

I don't go far, a couple of miles, before I'm into farm country. Small fields hemmed in by stone walls and rail fencing. Corrals of horses, the ground beneath them pummeled down to mud. The houses seem primitive, wood smoke rising from the chimneys. The asphalt road turns to gravel, and now I have to slow down and stop for some dangerous-looking cattle on the road. Massive, with long horns and shaggy coats, heads the size of wheelbarrows, they look like something out of the Ice Ages. As I inch forward among them, they dwarf the car, their wild eyes taking me in ominously.

In a yard nearby, a man in a straw hat is crouched over, pumping water—with a hand pump. Just as I emerge from the herd of cattle, he glances up. I wave—a gesture of reassurance, as I see it—but there's no way of telling from his expression what he thinks about that.

I continue driving, very slowly.

Ahead on the left, I see a girl approaching on the road, her hair covered with a blue scarf. She's walking alongside a pig, of all things, threatening its rump with a stick. The girl has an interesting face and—peeking out from under her scarf—red hair. What the heck, I roll the window down, and, as we pass one another, I say hello. But the pig, as you might expect, is making too damned much noise. She apparently doesn't hear me.

All this is frankly pretty astonishing. The scene, so near Brandewoode, seems impossibly rustic. I had no idea that any of this was here. Though I must admit that lately, outside of Argus Towers and Brandewoode and whatever's in between, I haven't been seeing a lot of the world. It has never even occurred to me, until now, to get out and explore the area, to just take a look at what's out here.

Well, now here I am.

I pass several other farms nestled in among tracts of woods. The odor of animals seems to have a cumulative effect. After awhile it's almost overpowering. The road deteriorates. Somewhere up ahead it must reemerge onto one of the highways near Brandewoode, but I've been on it for twenty minutes now, and I'm losing patience. I'm constantly steering around potholes, not to mention the droppings of some fairly large animals. It might be different if the people here were a little friendlier. Not that I really blame them. I can imagine they have better things to do than play up to people driving shiny new cars.

I look for a place to turn around. The chain, I suppose for the time being, can stay on the floor behind my seat. What the hell. Even if the police do stop me, it won't be the end of the world.

I am neither hungry nor thirsty, but I'm standing holding the fridge door open when Brenda enters the kitchen. She plucks the cork out of a bottle of Zinfandel, replenishes her glass, then turns to give me what feels like an appraisal. As if I were someone she hadn't seen in awhile. I stoop vaguely toward one of the middle shelves, my gaze sorting through the bottles there before finally homing in on the Worcestershire sauce. This may mark the first time I've had a use for the stuff.

It's a matter of only seconds. Brenda is on her way out of the kitchen when I hear myself say, "I took a different way home today."

"Oh?" She lingers at the hall. "What for?"

"I don't really know. Just a whim, I guess."

"That isn't like you, Michael."

I shrug. "Well, could be there's more to Michael than meets the eye."

She shifts her position, leaning against the wall, but she doesn't say anything.

"Yeah," I say, "I took a left off of seventeen. Brought me up into farm country."

"Farm country."

"Fields everywhere and fences and mud. I saw a girl herding a pig. At one point the entire road was blocked by cows. Or cattle, whatever they were. They looked like oxen."

"How could that be possible?"

"I'm only telling you what I saw."

"It's illegal, letting animals run over the road like that."

I would really like to think of something to say to her. But I've never been quick when it comes to talk.

I shut the fridge door. Time is running out. I say, "I've been thinking of maybe getting a boat."

This brings from Brenda a protracted, thoughtful stare.

"Michael," she says, "you're not going weird on me, are you?"

SATURDAY MORNING I'm up early. I dress, grab a little breakfast, and head out to the garage. Vince and I have arranged to go golfing today. This might not be so exciting in itself, but I haven't seen him for several days. I'm interested in finding out what's been bothering him.

Before lifting my bag into the trunk, I do a quick inventory: irons, woods, balls, shoes—everything is there.

Hearing a noise, I check out back. Swenson is there with an ax—already at this hour—limbing up some of the evergreens. There is authority in the crack of his ax strokes. I admire the way he handles the tool, with almost martial precision. I'll bet he keeps that blade sharp.

At the country club I don't see Vince's car. And the man himself is nowhere to be found. I check the locker room, the pool, the restaurant, and finally the front desk. No message. Then I happen to look at the calendar on the wall behind the desk. It's Sunday. I was supposed to meet Vince here yesterday! What happened to Saturday? I call Vince to apologize, but there's no answer. I'm probably just imagining it, but his voice on the voicemail recording seems angry. Who could blame him? I just hang up.

I go to the range, grab a bucket of balls, aiming to work on my slice. I take my time whacking them. When I've run out, I hit two more buckets. I try to focus. I try to stay calm. By the time I'm finished, I figure maybe I've got it under control. Then I think, who cares?

In the parking lot, loading my clubs into the trunk, I feel a sudden urge. I'd like to take off on my own and explore that farm country again. Maybe I could park somewhere, go for a walk. A hike even—it sounds crazy, but it provokes in me a slight adrenaline rush. God knows I can use it. I look down at the shoes I'm wearing—running shoes, I guess they are. Why wouldn't they be good enough? Maybe I'd have a new experience, something I could write a poem about. That girl with the red hair, I might run into her again.

Somehow on the highway I have a change of heart. I guess I lose my nerve. I don't make the turn. I just head home. Except that now there's this new thought: maybe I should write a poem.

In the driveway, getting out of the car, I happen to glance down at the floor behind the passenger seat, and—Jesus—I notice it's still there. The machete in its ornate leather scabbard. I forgot to take it out of the car. Which means I've been driving around with this thing for several days now. I open the back door, reach in, and grab it. Then I notice the chain. I consider taking that too, but it's all too much. I can come back for that later.

I have to say I'm impressed with the feel of the machete in my hand. There's a nice balance to it, something you seldom feel in a garden tool. It occurs to me, as long as Stan loaned it to me, I might as well try the thing on some weeds. It can't hurt. Preferably some time when Swenson isn't around.

As soon as I enter the kitchen, I realize something isn't right. It's as if I've been sleeping while something important was happening, and now suddenly I'm awake. I hold very still and listen. It's what I've been doing a lot of lately, it occurs to me, holding still and listening.

Somewhere there is a sound. I tiptoe out into the hallway. The sound is coming from upstairs. I'm fairly certain I recognize Brenda's voice. Then right away another sound, maybe another voice. I'm determined not to screw this up. This could be the opportunity I've been waiting for. Slowly, moving with the flow of the moment, I make my way to the stairs, then start up.

It's Brenda all right. She's talking intermittently, her voice almost a murmur. With every step, I focus, trying to judge the tone, trying to recognize a word. But there's too much carpet, a fan running somewhere. I can't make out anything she's saying. At the top of the stairs already I can see a little way into her studio.

I advance slowly to the doorway. The door is partly open. And—no need to open it the rest of the way—there they are in plain view. My Brenda and . . . Swenson. Yeah. My Brenda, stark naked. Swenson in his underwear, red and white boxer shorts, some sort of pattern. She's stooped over, showing him one of her paintings, one of her "works in progress." I don't know which one. I'm forbidden to see them. Anyway, I'm not looking at my wife's painting. My gaze is fixed instead on her nakedness, together with those hideous shorts of his. Swenson saying, "Hell, yah," in a quiet, almost tender voice. She giggles then, and he turns and lifts her clear up in the air, as if she weighed no more than an armful of crabapple twigs. Her smile beaming down at him, the toes of her naked foot nudge at the crotch of his shorts.

I'm witnessing all of this, standing there in the doorway with a machete in my hand. The machete, I understand, is as sharp as it is possible for a machete to be. This realization washes over me with a dreamlike lucidity.

At some point I'm aware that I'm in motion. I'm not making a sound. Or maybe I'm noisy and I just can't hear myself. It seems all at once, I'm down the stairs and out the door. Not the front door, but the back. I'm not making choices. It's all automatic. I'm not thinking about anything, except distance. All I know is I need to get away. I don't want to see anyone or talk to anyone. There is no time to waste. Any minute there could be wolves falling from the sky. Nothing would surprise me anymore. Nothing.

I'm across the lawn and barging off into the woods. It seems right somehow, original and careless. That trash marauder stalking the neighborhood?—give me a minute with him, me and my machete. Let the cops come after me with their guns. I guarantee, they've never seen anything like me.

It doesn't take long to find the trail. And then I'm off. I'm not quite running, not quite walking. Bounding is more like it. The trail winds, following the brook and threading its way between the massive, moss-covered trunks of the trees. And all the while, it seems, steadily climbing. Again it amazes me how far these woods extend. Given what I know of the layout of Brandewoode, I just don't see how it's possible. But here I am. So I wanted a hike, and now I have something better.

As I climb, I'm aware of the sound of the brook, the rush of blood in my ears, the ring of the machete blade against any sticks and brush that get in my way. At some point, stopping to rest, I hear something else. A rustling overhead, and then a branch snapping. I look up in time to see it fall—a small branch—missing me by inches. And at the same time, against the vast, luminous canopy of autumn-colored leaves, I catch a flash of something large and brown and—yes—hairy, flinging its way from limb to limb through the foliage. Not something you see every day. It's there, and then it's gone. "Hah!" I say out loud. My breathing quickens. My eyes are wide open. The world is close, very close. Inches from my face.

I'M PERCHED, cross-legged, on a big ledge overlooking a pool in the brook. The pool is deep, the water green, like the green of some storybook jewel. I think there might be fish in there, though I'm not sure. I can see shadows moving around. I had to scramble up in order to get here, bloodied my fingers and tore a rip in my pants. But I made it all right.

The brook cascading into the pool makes a dark, tantalizing sound. It's a little like water talking. So I'm sitting here, listening to it. I don't know yet what it's saying.

The rock I'm sitting on is coated all over with leathery moss-like stuff—pale green and gray, burgundy and brown, colors you wouldn't expect. And there are other rocks scattered around the forest floor like dice tossed by some giant. But mostly I'm surrounded by trees. I'm noticing now how many different kinds. I don't know the names. There are the evergreens with their needles, quite a few of those, and then—whatever they're called—the trees with leaves, rust-colored and brown and gold. Overall, the forest is mainly still, but every once in a while a leaf falls. The air hanging over the brook seems bright, restless in some way, as if it's about to become something else.

I look down at my clothes: running shoes and white slacks and mint-green golf shirt, all of it stained and sweaty, here and there a hole poked in the fabric. Remnants of my life, I guess you could say. My hair's probably a mess too, it's O.K. with me. I lean over to catch my reflection in the pool, but the light is wrong. There is no reflection.

Tired of carrying the scabbard around, I have threaded my belt through it, the way it's meant to be worn. I'm still holding on to the machete. It's true, I like the way it feels—the weight of it, the grip, and other sword-like qualities. I'm thinking this, sighting along the blade, when I notice it's aimed straight at the eyes of a dog across the brook. The animal is standing on the other side of the pool, half-hidden in some ferns, watching me. And now a second dog a little above him on the bank—he's watching me also.

Then I see the girl.

This time she's wearing some loose-fitting blouse, a skirt just above her knees, and what look like hiking boots—all of it gray, even the boots. But it's the same girl all right. Her eyes are on the machete, then on me. She says, "Are you on a hunting expedition?"

Her dogs intensify their stare, as though they, too, might be interested in the answer. I feel a wave of emotion rising, leftover from our last encounter, the one that left me screaming like a lunatic. The emotion begins as anger and then turns to something like shame.

"Oh, this?" I say. "This is for weeds."

She nods, skeptically.

Unless you count the ferns, of course there aren't any weeds on the forest floor, but I don't want to get into it.

She's searching me with those eyes.

I look away. It is becoming more and more apparent to me that the girl's face is in some way deformed. I'm avoiding looking at her directly, which makes it awkward since the two of us are facing one another utterly alone out here.

Not that her deformity, whatever it is, should make any difference to me. And I am only now understanding this. The fact is, thanks to my encounter with Brenda and Swenson, I feel (I don't know how else to describe it) somehow purified. What I remember of the old Michael—that flimsy bundle of fantasy, worry, and desire—has gone stale, lost its substance. I may need a shower, and my clothes may be filthy, but I feel essentially washed clean. Brenda?—Brenda who? Her looks?—what did they matter in the end? There I was, married to the most beautiful of women, who turned out to be a monster. What was my love for her, other than a pathetically overblown addiction? Well, no more.

No, yesterday I couldn't have imagined it. But today I am finally free. I'm sitting here, the new Michael, cleansed of those corrupt appetites and expectations, choosing to talk to this poor girl out walking her dogs. What better way to spend my time? What does it matter what she looks like?

I turn, lie back on the rock, and take a breath, staring up into the canopy of leaves overhead. "So," I say, "what are you doing out here, anyway? In the woods."

She steps away from the brook but remains standing, staring down at me, as though I'm the most interesting thing she's seen in a long time. "I live here," she says.

"What do you mean you live here?"

"At the edge of the meadow, just over that hill. It isn't far."

"Oh, in Brandewoode."

"What?"

Lying the way I am on the rock, I'm looking at her essentially upside down. She appears vaguely dwarf-like. It occurs to me, this topsy-turvy view may have something to do with our trouble communicating. I say, enunciating plainly, "You must live in Brandewoode."

"What's that?"

"Well . . . it's . . . It's where everybody around here lives. You know, the houses, the lawns." I'm wondering just how simple my talk has to become before she finally understands me. "Look, if you live here, you live in Brandewoode."

The girl just grins at me.

I'm beginning to think maybe she's a little weak in the head. And the prospect of dealing with that sort of person, well . . . . . I try a gentler tack. "I'm Michael," I say. "What's your name?"

"Grayce," she says. "With a Y."

I break into an upside-down chuckle. "How can you spell Grace with a Y?"

"G-R-A-Y-C-E."

"Oh."

It seems this Grayce can't take her eyes off me. I'm feeling a little self-conscious. I sit up a bit, prop myself on my elbows.

"You know," I say, "you need to be careful wandering around out here in these woods like this. It could be dangerous."

"True," she says. "All those weeds."

"No, listen. I'm serious. You don't know what sort of animal might be prowling around out here. Or some mental case."

"With a machete."

"Fine," I say. "Have it your way." Evidently there is no talking sense to this girl.

But now I notice something. What I first thought was a deformity appears instead to be jewelry—a rash of studs in her nose, and another cluster above the eyebrow. There are more, it seems, in her ear. The effect is unsettling, so much metal. It's awkward. I'd like to confront her, ask her why. Why she has, for all practical purposes, elected to live her life under the shadow of disfigurement. Is it the emblem of some society she belongs to? A kind of religious penance? But of course I can't ask any of this. No, even the new Michael doesn't have that kind of nerve. Who knows how she'd react. Her two dogs are still silently eyeing me.

I say, "Those are pretty big dogs."

"They aren't dogs," she says. "They're wolves."

"Oh, really?" I sit up a little straighter on the ledge. "I didn't know you could make wolves into pets."

"Who says they're pets."

To which I don't say anything. I'm twisted around, looking at her over my shoulder now, feeling the effect of her eyes. And then there are the eyes of those animals of hers, whatever they are. A constellation of eyes, all watching me.

"Come on," she says. She turns and dashes away up the trail.

I'm on the verge of saying something, registering an objection. But what? Across the brook, her wolves have vanished with her. What the hell, I get up and follow.

It's hard keeping up with her, never mind the wolves. Ahead every so often, through the tree-trunks and rocks and fern, I can see the flutter of that skirt just above her knees. God, she's quick! Then I completely lose sight of her.

Of course, I'm not ruling out the possibility that it's just another stupid prank. She could be right at this moment hiding in the brush along the trail, watching me struggle past for her own amusement. But I go ahead and struggle anyway, machete in hand. It's not as if I have anything better to do.

I've already slowed to a walk. After maybe half a mile, the path opens onto a clearing, and there the girl is standing in front of the damnedest living quarters I've ever seen. The place looks exactly like a gypsy wagon, complete with—believe it or not—spoked wheels. I approach, somewhat doubtfully, until I'm standing right next to her.

The wolves are nowhere to be seen.

It occurs to me that I'm still holding the machete. I take a moment to sheathe the blade in its scabbard. We're both standing there, looking at the wagon. It's painted in what once may have been bright colors—purple, yellow, and green, though faded now and grown over with moss. All except for the door, a warm red, which appears to have been very recently redone. In fact, leaning in for a closer look, I'd swear the paint on the door seems still wet.

I'm dumbfounded.

She hops up, opens the little door to the trailer, and disappears inside. Then she pokes her head back out. She says, "You want to come in?"

Something about the situation raises my suspicions.

"You live here?" I say.

"Yeah. I told you."

The fog brightens and darkens erratically as we talk. The reflections off the metal on the girl's face complicate her expression, suggesting here a smile and there a frown where in fact there may be neither.

I'm fingering the hilt of the machete. There's a certain feel to it, the way it rides on my hip. I'd say, almost warrior-like. It's probably ageless, this feeling. In some odd way, my hand on this weapon, I could imagine myself gazing down through centuries, time simply dissolving.

I'm standing there, looking up at her. I've been invited inside.

"But I don't understand," it occurs to me to say. "How did this get here?"

"I brought it in, hitched it up to my horse."

"What horse?"

"Zoroaster. He died." She casts a glance over my head, apparently across the meadow. Her expression may be one of sadness. Or maybe something over there at the edge of the woods has caught her attention. She adds in a faraway voice, "That was a long time ago."

"I'm sorry to hear that," I say. But I'm not sure she's listening.

"So," she says, "are you coming in?"

I don't even really consider it. From where I'm standing, I can't see very far into the interior of that wagon. It seems awfully dark in there, even though the little place has plenty of windows.

"No, that's all right," I say. "I should really be getting back. It's probably pretty late."

For an instant, around her mouth, it seems there's a flicker of hurt. I can't be sure.

"But it is a really nice place you have," I say. I feel awkward.

She's looking at me with the expression of someone trying to decipher the speech of a crazy person.

"I've enjoyed talking with you," I say, raising my voice a bit, trying to force some sense into what I'm saying. I look around, then offer a little wave, the kind supposed to signal the end of a conversation.

Straightening, she shakes her head, ducks back inside, and briskly shuts the door.

I feel immediately guilty. It seems, out of sheer clumsiness, I may have actually injured the girl's feelings. I'd be half-ready to knock on the door with some demonstration of kindness, if she hadn't shut it with such finality. Then, too, there's the wet paint.

I turn and head down the trail. Back toward . . . God knows what. I don't even want to think about it.

At the edge of the meadow I look back. From the roof of the little gypsy trailer I see a rusty smokestack protruding, out of which is rising a thin column of smoke. Poor kid. I wonder whose property she's camped out on.

A Margin of Safety

THIS IS WHAT we're told. And then, as if by magic, we see it. Somewhere, somehow deep underground, there is a fire burning endlessly. It isn't far from where we're standing now, here among these ancient trees. The fire, raging through a network of furnace-like caverns, has been burning over a very long time.

On the slopes and ridges above a certain glade of dark reputation, we are told, the forest floor is honeycombed with openings, subterranean vents that flare like nostrils, sucking air and emitting smoke. In this way, on windless days when the trees are still (as they are today), one can hear the fire down below, breathing. More than that—over the years, a bright and roughly textured moss the color of cinnabar has spread from these holes like wildfire, blanketing everything at ground level and threatening to paint its way up the trunks of trees. A sharp odor hangs in the air, like sulfur. Like heat. Like the memory of combustion itself. All the forest is alert to this. Jay and wren and goshawk eying things from spruce limbs. Fox and vole and weasel and deer picking their way through underbrush—all in their separate ways know about the fire.

It isn't fear that they carry, but more like a blind and pure attention. More like another thing to step around. They don't avoid those orifices in the ground. But nearing them, they move more perfectly, knowing they're on the very edge of something.

Even here, trying to slough it off, still we feel the ground trembling. What is rampaging down there seems one long contained explosion, burning as if forever. Heat beyond imagining. Chamber after chamber cascading liquid fire. What could ever hold it? What is it that burns if not the earth itself? Hidden away in pockets among the magma, the coals and gases compress into orange-yellow clustering shapes. There they flicker and scintillate like dramas, like pitched campaigns, like worlds sculpted out of fire alone.

BACK AT THE HOUSE, Brenda is gone. The front door is wide open. Her car isn't in the garage. There's no sign of Swenson or his truck. Maybe they've eloped. I'm a little disappointed. I'm not sure why.

Well, anyway, here I am. I hoist myself up on the kitchen counter and sit there. It's a view of the kitchen I've never had before, and it makes the kitchen seem like something else, something I should have recognized long ago.

Upstairs I go from room to room. At each window I stand, listening. I walk right into Brenda's studio. One by one, I look at all her paintings, every last one of them. Another disappointment. I look around at everything in the room, nodding.

In the bedroom I take my time getting out of my clothes, making a pile of them on the floor. I consider tossing them all in the trash. The garbage marauder is welcome to them. He can eat them, for all I care. Then, gathering them up, I change my mind. The stains, the holes—the truth is I'm not quite ready to give these up. I hang the shirt and pants on hangers, separately against the closet doors. Like art. Why not? The running shoes—well, I'll think of something.

From the bathroom mirror my face looks back at me, apparently puzzled by what it sees. My growth of beard is a day-and-a-half old—the longest it's ever been. I keep rubbing my hand over it. I can feel the urge of temptation rising inside me.

In the shower I remember the doors to the house are open, front and back—not to mention the windows. Anything could get in here. So I crack open the shower glass door enough to look out. The machete is there in its scabbard, close by, hanging from the towel rack. I'm not taking any chances.

While I'm drying off, I can hear birds singing somewhere out in the yard. I wonder what kind. I don't know much about birds. I can spot a robin on the lawn. And a cardinal. But what they sound like? I'm at a loss.

Downstairs I open a Corona and make myself a sandwich. I switch on the TV, turn it to the news. The excitement is all about the hurricane churning up the East Coast. Hurricane Luther—a monster, from the look of him, flooding rivers, crumpling telephone poles, blowing the roofs off gymnasiums. An erratic storm, they're emphasizing, meandering its way here tomorrow or the day after. They can't be sure. And here I've forgotten all about it. It looks as if I'll have to close some windows. I go to the living room picture window, peer out at the tops of the trees, but everything looks calm. I switch to the weather channel. Then the phone rings.

It's Stan. I'm surprised to hear his voice.

"Hey," I say, "What's up?"

"We're down here," he says. "You want to come and see her?"

"Down where? See who?"

"My boat, man."

Out front on Forest Drive I see a police car cruise by, slowly.

Stan's voice says, "We're down here at the pier. Come on down."

"What pier?"

"Goose Harbor. It's not far."

"I don't know where that is. I never heard of it."

"So use a map."

There is hesitation on my part. The fact is, at this very moment, I'm watching a boat on the TV screen. The boat, beneath a wildly flailing set of traffic lights, is crushing a car.

Stan's voice says, "Look, it's three and a half miles off of 15. It won't take you half an hour."

Which is how I find myself in the car on this obliterated Sunday afternoon, heading vaguely for the ocean. I'm aware of a dumb incandescence blistered into my memory where Sunday morning should be. It is there all right, there is no denying it. What

I'm supposed to do with it is another matter. I have the map spread out on the passenger seat.

I don't get far before I'm interrupted. Already at the corner of Dogwood, I can see a police car and two Brandewoode Security vehicles parked in front of the Brennans' house, half a block away. A BWS guard stationed in the middle of the road is slowing the cars that pass and looking in their interiors before waving them on. As he leans stern-faced and peers into my window, I feel a twinge of anxiety. Apparently, though, he doesn't notice the chain. Up on the Brennans' lawn by the corner of the house near some flower beds I see Jim Kincaid, two police officers, and a guard all standing, staring down at something. Gently, gently I step on the gas.

Maybe a hundred feet up the road, Betty Johnson is standing at the edge of her lawn like a statue, a sweater draped over her shoulders.

I stop, roll the window down. I ask her what's up.

"Harry," she says, without taking her eyes from the Brennans'.

I shake my head.

She nods meaningfully. "Just like Mel."

"My God," I say.

"Early this morning. He went out to get the paper." She nods. "Just the way Mel did."

"Heart attack?"

"If that's what they want to call it." She leans in close to the window, maybe a little too close. She lowers her voice. "Jo said he looked like he'd seen the devil."

I turn my head again toward the police and Jim Kincaid, where now from this angle I can see something by the flower bed—maybe Harry Brennan's shoe.

"This is not normal, what's going on," Betty says. "Say what you want. This is not normal."

My hands clamped tight on the steering wheel, I weigh these words of Betty's. I stare hard out the windshield, the direction that seems to be coming next.

In spite of the map, I get slightly lost. Stan's half hour turns into forty-five minutes. Partly I'm distracted, continually looking up at where the sky ought to be. Though of course there is no sky because the fog is in the way. All this talk about the weather has me spooked. There is a peculiar deadness to the air. Hurricane Luther, I'm thinking, what a name! The storm of the century, they're calling it. I have to think of that poor woman, Grayce, stuck way out in a meadow in her tiny gypsy wagon. I can't imagine that roof would keep water off. You hear now and then about the underprivileged, but, practically speaking, you hardly ever meet up with one of them. I feel a surge of sympathy for her, all that metal in her face. Now there's a clear case of one bad choice after another.

Then all of a sudden it occurs to me, I could invite Grayce to the house! Offer to let her ride the storm out there. Let's see how Brenda would like that.

Finally I see a sign to Goose Harbor, and a minute later I'm on the waterfront, parking the car. The place is busy, people yanking small boats out of the water. The fog here has a different feel to it. It takes me awhile, plodding up and down the pier, trying to spot Stan and trying to imagine what his boat looks like, before I eventually hear his voice. I turn, and there he is on the deck of a boat so big that I didn't even see it. A sleek, black sailboat, the thing has to be fifty feet long. I don't know the first thing about boats, but this one looks in great shape. Standing next to him is a woman with green hair, smiling. Dolores.

"What are you doing?" I yell.

Stan just grins. On the deck close by, two little girls are running around in circles and bashing their heads against Stan's legs. "Come on aboard," he yells. He points to a ramp leading from the pier to the boat.

On board he and Dolores show me around. The kids tag along, running insane circles around us. The boat is a sloop, Dolores says as we head down some stairs. Below deck, they take me through a suite of cabin rooms, Stan mumbling the names of things. "Galley. Hatchway. Sleeping quarters." Though I can tell in that mumbling there's a kind of pride. We come to what he calls "The Blitz Room," full of technical hardware: computer, satellite, radar, sonar, GPS, radio equipment, who knows what else. There's room enough down here in the hold, Dolores tells me, to store provisions for several months at sea.

"Head's in there," Stan mumbles, pointing to a door.

The boat is beautiful. Whatever isn't brass or natural wood is painted black or green or red. I look at everything.

Stan uses his sleeve to rub the tarnish off a doorknob. He mumbles, "You could sail around the world on this baby."

I wait till we get back up on deck and we've all taken a breath before I ask, "But do you know how to work this thing?"

Dolores, it turns out, has done some sailing. The past few weeks, she's been showing him things. But Stan only finally bought the boat today.

I look up into the fog. "What about the hurricane?"

"Not a problem in this harbor," Dolores says.

I'm in no position to argue with her. I'm standing on the deck, my hands in my jacket pockets. Throwing my head back, trying to take in the top of the mast, I feel like I'm falling over backwards. I could imagine we're in another time.

"Stan," I say.

"Pow!" one of the little girls yells, ramming her head against Stan's legs. Stan rocks a little sideways. He looks as if he couldn't be happier.

I look around, shake my head.

"What?" he says.

"How? I mean . . . how?"

He shrugs.

I say, "If you don't mind my asking. I mean, this is a millionaire's boat. Are you getting a promotion?"

"Nah, I sold the house."

"You what?"

"Carlson is fixing to can me."

"Not possible," I say.

"I don't know when exactly, but I'm sure it's coming. That guy Folsom has me in his sights."

"I don't know about that."

"Mark my word."

"But Stan. Your place? You sold your place?"

"Yeah."

"You loved that place."

"Yeah, the hell with it."

"The hell with it," one of the little girls says, standing still now, looking up at me.

Stan chuckles, ruffles her hair.

I shake my head. I don't know what to say.

"God's sake, Michael," Stan says, "it's just a house."

"Yeah, but . . . what are you going to do?"

"Live on my boat."

"Wow. You sold your house." I say it again. I feel a little foolish repeating it, but each time it comes out a little differently, I'm hoping closer to the meaning. But the meaning isn't cooperating. It might as well be hiding, somewhere out there in the fog.

By the time I get back to the car, I'm chilled to the bone from all that standing around in the cold air. In a way, those little girls knew what they were doing, running, keeping the blood pumping. I turn the heater on high. I watch the signs now, trying not to get lost on the way back. But there's too much on my mind, distracting me. Twice I wind up on the wrong road. Then again, what difference does it make? Whether I get lost.

I'm thinking back. One thing I did notice. She has nice-looking knees, that Grayce.

ON THE WAY HOME I'm delayed at three separate roadblocks, two just in Brandewoode. Each time, the police ask for my license, registration, proof of insurance. I can't help wondering, don't they ever tire of this? They orbit the car, leer into the interior. At the second roadblock, my officer buddy Tom asks me sternly, "You got any poetry in the trunk?"

I hesitate.

His face wrinkles then. I guess it's a smile. He doesn't say anything else, just slaps the roof of my car and waves me on.

Pulling into the driveway, I see Brenda's car in the garage. Now there we go. I'm wondering what it will be like, our confrontation.

But there is no confrontation. I'm standing in the kitchen, the fridge door open, a bottle of apple juice in my hand when I hear her footsteps coming up the stairs from the basement. At the top of the stairs she glances my way, shuts the basement door, and switches off the light. She has something under her arm—a roll of canvas.

Pausing before heading off down the hall, she asks, "How was golfing?"

Somewhere in the distance there is the sound of a siren.

"Golfing was great." I'm looking around the kitchen. Maybe there's something to go with apple juice. "I smacked the goddamned piss out of those balls," I say, giving a hearty emphasis to the word "piss."

She holds her ground, tilts her head quizzically. "Are you O.K.?" she says.

"Fuck, I'm . . . ." I mean to say "superb," but instead it comes out "superfluous." I give a short laugh.

She nods uncertainly.

I hold her in a profound stare. "Are you ready for the hurricane, Brenda?"

She just gawks at me. It's a first for me, seeing Brenda gawk.

I wag my finger at her. "You don't *look* ready."

Before she has a chance to answer, there is a loud knock at the door. Another first—not in all the years we've lived here have I ever heard that. Then, as if it were an afterthought, the doorbell rings.

Brenda goes to answer it.

I open one of the overhead cabinets, pull down a box of spiced vegetable crackers. Over the rattle of the cellophane as I'm grabbing a handful, I hear a voice from the front hall. I hold the box quiet enough to recognize Jim Kincaid's voice. He's probably here, I figure, to warn us about the hurricane.

But no, when I go to join the conversation, I discover Jim has other business on his mind. Standing just inside the door, his hand poised on the knob, he's dressed as neatly as a hotel doorman, but without the hat. His shoes are polished, his slacks creased, his uniform jacket zipped to chest level. Strapped to his belt is some sort of radio-pager gizmo, which now and then crackles with noise.

"Mr. Benson, Sir," he says, "I apologize for interrupting your evening." His tone sounds somehow insincere, perhaps even mocking.

I, for one, am in no mood to be mocked. "Not a problem," I say. "Would you like a cracker?" I offer him the box.

"No, no. No thanks. I was just informing your wife, we expect to be engaging in a series of investigations over the next couple of days."

Brenda's interest quickens. "Are these connected with the . . . ?"

"Yes, well, that, and we've had a couple of other incidents. One not far from here, over in the vicinity of Hawthorne Lane."

I notice Brenda nodding. I offer her the crackers, but she waves them away.

"Trash-related?" I say.

Brenda throws me a look of impatience.

"Beg your pardon?" Jim Kincaid says.

"Do these incidents involve the pilfering of anyone's garbage?"

Jim seems wary of the question. "No," he says. "Not to my knowledge."

"Hm!" I say.

"In any case," Jim says, "we'll be making every effort not to get in anyone's way."

Cracking the door a bit wider, he seems ready to make his exit. But then, leaning in Brenda's direction, he adds in a confidential tone, "We've been a little short-staffed over the years. Luckily now they've upped the budget. We've expanded the force, brought three new vans into play. Fully-surveillance-equipped." He aims this last information at me, before turning again to Brenda. "Not to worry, though. We'll mostly be out of sight. Reconnoitering the woods, I expect."

"The woods?" I say.

"If you see us at all, it'll probably be crossing your yard with the dogs."

"Why the woods?"

Jim, focused on matters of staff efficiency, seems not to hear the question. "They'll be done before you even know they're there."

"I don't know," I say. "It seems pretty unlikely to me that these woods could have anything at all to do with it. I mean, heart attacks."

Brenda turns and looks at me as if I were crazy.

Jim shakes his head. "Well, there isn't much to these woods, it's true. On the other hand, if someone were looking for a place to hide . . . ." He pushes the door open and steps outside onto the stoop. "Anyway . . . that's all I wanted to tell you, really. You see anything that's not right, you give us a call."

"Thanks for the warning," Brenda says.

"Not a thing to worry about, I'm sure," he says. He flips us a little three-fingered salute, then turns and descends our granite front steps.

I stand holding the box of crackers, watching Jim's polished shoes click their way down our walk. There is something about the sound of those shoes that I don't like, any more than I like the idea of Brandewoode Security running one of their dragnets through these woods, where they're sure, it seems, to snag poor Grayce. It crosses my mind that she ought to be warned. On the one hand, it would look bad if I were caught sneaking around out there where, let's face it, I have no business to be. It was only a couple of days ago they stopped me with that machete. I wouldn't want to establish a pattern. On the other hand, the woman is perfectly harmless. They get one look at that face jewelry, and they're certain to yank her out of that gypsy wagon of hers and haul her off to some mental institution.

I shove the front door closed. Brenda meanwhile has disappeared with her roll of canvas. I glance upstairs, where she probably went. For a moment I'm tempted to follow her there, swagger into her studio, ambush her in a discussion of her "works in progress," not the least of which involves our upstart gardener. Oh, excuse me, forester. I'd like to see the reaction assemble on that exquisite face of hers. But really that all seems unnecessary. Her paintings simply don't interest me. And as for her escapades with the hired help, I'd sooner keep that in reserve, like a grenade in my pocket, ready to use whenever the moment seems ripe.

Right now, instinct tells me, I have better things to do. I'm not sure yet what those are. But I like the feel of looking around, noticing what's here. We walk through this world—I'm coming to understand—and either we see things or we don't. Lately, I'll tell you, I've been getting an eyeful.

I feel the urge to be free of encumbrances. I set the box of crackers and then the juice bottle on the stairs. I consider removing my clothes, stripping myself stark naked. But, no, I suspect it's been done before. There must be other possibilities. More profound.

I can see through the windows, daylight is fading outside. Maybe the fog is thickening. Or maybe somewhere—I can barely imagine it—the sun is setting. In here now, the space of the hallway seems largely in shadow. I make no move, though, to switch on a light. Trusting to native cunning, I wander into the dining room. There is something about this room that is continually drawing me back. And now I know what it is.

No more than a quick glance around, then without a thought I pull out a chair and step on it. The next thing I know I'm up standing on the table. The diningroom table! Square in the center, just like on a big walnut surfboard. Just like on a fresh plane of existence. That's what it's like exactly. One foot forward and one back, my arms extending out for balance, I'm riding the great wave of this house.

"Hah!" I yell.

I feel things shaking. I hear Brenda's voice, a little involuntary squeak.

Brenda and her paintings, my golf clothes hanging, all these wallpapered rooms, separate from one another, windows open and closed—who can say what's getting in or out?—the whole goddamned circus collapsing, pitching forward, and I'm riding it.

> One by one, the hours expire
> And drop away, slackening your fingers.
> Even the sky collapses,
> Letting in the thick, black winds of gravity.
> The ground—feel it! slithering your heels—
> Rises and curls.
> So many lost and unsuspected reasons,
> Left and right, ascend and veer,
> Swarm on their new wings.
> Flung like this, you wonder
> Whether you have ever known the world
> And whether after all it could be friendly.

The words, O.K., they seem to make no sense, but at times like this there's no stopping them.

"Hah!!" I yell it again, even louder. Everything tumbling forward. Toward what?

WHEN I OPEN my eyes the following morning, I'm lying in the hammock on the screen porch. I'm not sure how I got here. Outside, the fog has vanished. Gone! I can see things. There's a strong wind in the trees.

I look out through the mesh of the screen at a sky churning gray. I remember several times in the night being awakened by noises I've never heard before. The noises seemed to come from the woods. Each time I fell back to sleep.

This is another way, I think, nodding as though in agreement. This is another way for a day to begin.

In the kitchen, throwing together some breakfast, suddenly I'm aware of a muffled rumbling. Out in the yard the rain is so heavy I can hardly see the flower beds. Gusts are hurling rain against the windows and the side of the house.

A few minutes later I'm standing in the hall, just inside the front door, listening. I turn the knob, push the door open a crack, then wide. I venture out onto the stoop, my cereal bowl in my upturned palm. The wind rushes across the lawn, lifts at my hair, and flaps my clothes around. I'm spooning wet, crunchy cereal into my mouth, watching the trees rock back and forth, their trunks surprisingly flexible. The rain seems to have stopped. The air is swarming with wet leaves and bits of grass and who knows what else. As they swirl around, some of these things hit my face. I'm nodding, tasting the cereal. There's no denying, it's all happening.

"Luther," I say out loud. I thrust my spoon in the air.

An abrupt, powerful gust nearly knocks me off the stoop.

"That's right!" I say, steadying myself against the clapboards. Talking to a hurricane. And getting answers. All of this bears watching. Somewhere in the back of my mind I understand, things are taking on new shapes. The wind is roaring, of course I haven't forgotten that. More than once, between spoonfuls of cereal, my hand goes up to my face. I can feel the growth of beard there, spreading like a lawn. Soon enough, like a meadow.

Upstairs I shower and dress for work, the way I always do. I don't shave. Into my pockets go my wallet and keys, along with the little notebook I carry now. I've been having ideas again. Brenda, in bed, is sleeping late, the way she always does. The bedroom window is open to the storm. Knotting my tie, I can see in the mirror the curtains billowing into the room, like in a haunted-house movie. But then the rain begins again, and I have to close the window—a little too noisily, I guess, because it wakes Brenda.

She rises on her elbows, squints out at the rain. "What are you doing?" she says.

"I'm going to work."

She looks at me. "Are you out of your mind?"

I don't answer this.

I watch her get out of bed. She slips into a robe.

"Michael," she says with finality, "everything is shut down today."

I regard her doubtfully.

She runs her fingers through her hair, then adds, "This close to the coast, they're talking of evacuating for Christ's sake."

A blast of rain draws her attention to the window.

It is mainly the calm in my voice, I think, that brings her back. "I take it you're the storm expert then, Brenda? Been doing a bit of research on it, have you? In bed, with your eyes closed?"

"Michael, what has gotten into you?"

I don't answer this either.

But then I think, what the hell, I'll give it one try. "Look, Brenda," I say, "we run around, thinking we have it all figured out, intending this or that. Only to discover, life has other plans."

Brenda snatches her comb off the bureau. "Life doesn't plan," she says. "It strikes."

And as if to confirm the truth of her words, a gust of wind shakes the house.

"Tell me," she says. "What possible justification could you have for driving out into a category-five hurricane?"

"I don't know how else to explain it. I feel the need."

She looks at me as though she didn't hear me, as though I haven't yet answered her. Then she turns, heads toward the bathroom. "You forgot to shave," she says.

By the time I back the car out of the garage, the rain has let up again. Even the wind seems to have calmed. Perhaps the reports of the storm are exaggerated. Perhaps it has decided to pass us by, slip out to sea, the way hurricanes do. But on the highway it's another story. Even with the wipers on high, the windshield looks like I'm driving underwater. The steering wheel yanks at my grip like something recklessly alive. I slow to forty miles an hour, then thirty-five, then thirty. Ahead, police and ambulance lights riot through the blur of the windshield—an accident. Then another, a couple of miles further, a car upside down on the side of the road. The police haven't arrived. They may not even know about this one. I consider stopping, but too late, after I've already passed.

I'm watching for my exit, but it isn't easy. The rain is so thick, I can't read signs. The highway looks entirely strange. There is something beyond the wind and the rain, some sort of darkness over things. Finally I see what looks like an exit. It seems somehow right, and I veer into it. I'm driving twenty miles an hour now, my face thrust up against the windshield. At the bottom of the exit ramp there's a light pole angling across the road, but I manage to steer around it. I make the left onto Kingsbury, an avenue normally choked with traffic but now deserted. The rain thins again. I keep an eye out for Argus Towers, half-expecting the wind has blown it over. But a few minutes later there it is, that white monolith, solid under the dark sky.

The parking lot is practically empty—a few cars, none of them occupied, as far as I can tell. I sit in the car with the engine running, waiting. Maybe soon someone else will show: Wendel Carlson, Vince. I look at the cars again, more carefully. There are, altogether, four—not counting mine. Three of them I don't recognize. But the fourth one, sure enough, is a black Mercedes. Somewhere up in that tower Jack Folsom is slowly pacing a carpet.

Sitting at a desk. Opening drawers, going through someone's file cabinet. There's no telling what he's up to.

I hesitate, then shut the engine off, grab my umbrella, and brace myself. With the wind pressing against the door, I have to shove hard to open it. But then—all, it seems, in one move—I'm out and running with the umbrella open. If you could call it running, the whole way fighting the umbrella.

And then—of all things!—I almost step on a snake. The thing is wriggling, maybe swimming, vaguely upwind through the water in the parking lot. I don't have much further to go, though, before I'm under the shelter of the building entrance, with nothing worse than damp clothes and soaked shoes. I fold the umbrella.

I try the door, which, O.K., is locked. That much I might have guessed. I knock against the glass with the umbrella handle to attract someone's attention, but in the noise of the storm it's hopeless. I can barely hear the knock myself. For some reason I have to think of Brenda now at home. Maybe still in her robe, but probably back in bed. Whatever she's wearing, whatever she's doing, she doesn't know about this—that's plain enough—me locked out, the wind blowing up my trousers and howling around the mouth of Argus Towers, as though the building has been mortally wounded. She hasn't the slightest idea. No. You can't sleep your way into a chowder like this.

Out there beyond the entrance, things are happening—things you don't normally see. The wind is sucking up clumps of bark chips from the gardens by the hedges, flinging them across the walk. To the left I hear a loud crack, and an aluminum light pole leans and crashes to the asphalt not twenty feet from Jack's Mercedes. Out on Kingsbury through a break in the rain I see the flashing lights of an ambulance, moving slowly, like something that has lost its way.

I'm contemplating my car, no more than fifty feet away, when something flying-saucer-like screams past my ear and rings against the building wall. It caroms, chipping a concrete pillar, and spins away again into the storm. A hubcap maybe.

It occurs to me that, all things taken into account, I have seen enough. And at exactly that moment I see something more—on the concrete around the building entrance, more snakes. Two of them coiled in a corner. Another slithering by the door. That's it. I'm running for the car. I'm almost there when the wind switches and gusts, catching the umbrella. It pretty near rips my arm off, spinning me around, and the next thing I know, I'm sprawled beside the island curb, lying in half an inch of water, watching the umbrella sailing—ten, fifteen feet off the ground now—across the parking lot.

In the car I assess the damage: the front of my suit is wet, so are my shoes and socks. My hands are a bit scraped, and I've lost my umbrella. Otherwise I'm O.K. I start the car, turn the wipers on.

Back on Kingsbury, I'm headed home the way I came. I'm crawling now, threading around obstacles. Rain is exploding in gusts against the passenger windows. A green plastic lawn chair, driven like tumbleweed, smashes into my right fender and flips over the hood of the car, just missing the windshield. Noticing suspicious movement a hundred feet ahead, I stop in time to watch the red-white-and-blue roof of a gas station carport summersault in slow motion across the road. I wait for it, respectfully, the way I might wait for a funeral procession to pass. Rain is hammering the car until it seems the window might break. Inside the glass, water is dribbling from the seams.

"Luther," I say. My voice has lost some of its cockiness.

I keep an eye on the sky, remembering flying boats.

On the highway, where it's lined with trees, the wind isn't as bad. I see headlights—a car, then a second, both headed in the opposite direction. The second one flashes its brights—some kind of signal. I slow down, maneuver around a tree lying across the road. Half a mile beyond that, I brake for red and blue flashing lights. Some sort of cop in a yellow rain coat is standing in the lee of a fire truck, motioning for me to turn around, go back.

I roll my window down.

He has his slicker hood up so I can't see his face, but I can hear him well enough. "Road's blocked!" he screams. He motions again for me to turn around.

I yell, "What about Route 3?"

His whole upper body swivels in the negative. "No idea!" he screams.

I roll the window up, turn the car around, and head back the way I came. "Jesus, Luther," I say, "you know how to play hard ball."

A sharp gust muscles the car sideways, scooting it onto the gravel shoulder.

"Whoa!" I say. I slow to ten miles an hour. There must be other ways home, but I've never driven any of them. Under the circumstances, I can barely recognize the roads I know. And those other roads could be blocked too.

I'm nearly on top of it when I suddenly realize—that high road through the meadow! If I follow it far enough, it ought to come out somewhere near Brandewoode.

I make the turn and begin the climb away from the highway. The wind, if anything, is even wilder up here across the meadow, shoving the car around. But I'm getting more or less used to it, and at the speed I'm driving, I can't get into much trouble. Of course, it's tedious going. With the windshield wipers pounding back and forth, I'm passing the same farmhouses, the same animal pens and fields, or at least what I can see of them through the water-coated windows, though everything does look different, sort of pulled into itself, like a turtle into its shell. Beyond the farms the road passes through wooded sections and then finally turns to dirt. Or I should say mud. I can feel the car slow and wander as the wheels contend with the slip and slide. But soon I get the hang of it. It's a question of momentum, of staying on the inside of curves and not letting the wheels spin too much. Here in the woods at least the wind isn't so bad.

I'm doing it, I keep repeating to myself. Whatever happens, I'm doing it.

Now the road descends, and I've got my fingers crossed. It ought to be close to the end by now. It ought to be spilling soon into Brandewoode.

But the road narrows further. The canopy of trees closes in, making it harder to see. The grade turns steep and now cuts sharply left. There's no question about it, the car is sliding. I gear down and correct the steering, but I'm not in control. The brakes are too late. As the car drifts to a stop, I feel it tilt. The rear passenger wheel slumps into a ditch.

I try in low gear easing the car forward, but with each attempt there's less movement. One of the front wheels is spinning, digging itself a hole.

Finally I don't do anything. I just sit there, waiting for my mind—which seems to have continued down that mud road—to stop and turn around and come back for me. "All right," I say out loud, "why?"

All I knew this morning was that I wasn't going to wait this storm out with Brenda, in that house. Which doesn't explain—does it?—why I'm trying so hard to get home now. So here I am, sitting, peering out through a windshield plastered with leaves. I make a fist, contemplate pounding it against the steering wheel, but where's the advantage in that? I shut the wipers off, at least I'm rid of that noise.

Jesus, the woods are dark. I'm miles, it seems, from anywhere. There's practically nobody out in this storm but me. I suppose, if worst comes to worst, I could ride it out here. Like a bug in a bottle.

Then I remember the chain, still lying on the floor behind my seat. What about it? If I could weave that chain back and forth underneath the tire that's spinning, that might give it the traction it needs. The thought of putting that chain to practical use almost perks me up. The damned thing's been nothing to me so far but an embarrassment.

At the moment it's pouring rain, but that's not going to stop me. I get out and start around the car to look things over. And, first thing, before anything else, I have to jump to avoid stepping on a snake. God, is there anyplace free of them? This is a big one, too, maybe five feet long. Iridescent green, slithering off underneath the car. I look around for others, but all I see are leaves and rain and mud.

As for the car, the situation doesn't look too bad. It's the driver's side wheel that's spinning. The ditch isn't all that deep. If the tire tread catches on the chain, I might be able to ride out on it. I open the back door, reach in behind the seat, and grab the chain. The thing is heavy—I've forgotten how heavy. I remember when I bought it—not that long ago really—with Ted standing right there. I have to wonder how, at this very moment, old Ted is doing.

It's still raining heavily. With every step my shoes are sinking an inch or two into the mud. I'm soaked to the skin, but who cares? At least I don't have to worry about getting wet. I shut the back door and slog my way around to the front tire. I'm leaning to lay the chain, keeping my eyes peeled for snakes, when past the fender, I see something through the trees—a light of some kind. It's not on the road, apparently, but off in the woods. I straighten up, take a couple of steps, squinting at it through the rain. The beam appears to be flickering on and off like some sort of signal. But, no—when I move closer, I realize it's a steady light. It's only that I'm seeing it through the churn of vegetation. There might be a house, maybe another road, someone with a four-wheel drive. I don't hesitate. I head for it.

I wind up staggering through the woods, frankly maybe a little punchy. The wet clothes are beginning to sap the heat out of me. I can't see very well. I get whacked in the face a couple of times by branches. But soon enough I arrive at the edge of a clearing. And, incredible as it seems, I'm standing smack in front of that woman's gypsy wagon. Little Grayce. That's where the light is coming from, inside her windows. Amazing.

I'm standing there, shaking my head. Sure, I have mixed feelings about presenting myself at her door, given the dimensions of the mess I'm in, the pure humiliation of it. On the other hand, I can't stay out in this rain much longer. And there seems—though my thinking is fuzzy here—a certain logic to my being here, a certain inevitability. What the hell.

I step up onto the wrought-iron stair and deliver four sharp knocks on her newly-red-painted door. And in spite of the noise of the storm, I hear her voice—unmistakable—from inside. "Come on in!" it says. There is not a suggestion of misgiving in that voice, as if it were more or less to be expected that in the midst of a hurricane someone should show up at her door deep in the woods. So I enter.

Grayce, wearing her same gray skirt and blouse, is nestled in a corner, where she has been reading a book, it looks like. Her wolves are lying at her feet like bookends, one on either side of her. There's a fire going in a wood stove. The place is lit by candle and kerosene lantern. It's cozy.

"Hey!" she says when she sees me. Then, "Oh, you brought me a present."

I look down to where the chain, covered with mud, is double-draped over my shoulder.

She snaps her book closed and bounces to her feet. "You carried that thing all the way up here? It's a nice gesture, really it is, but would you mind leaving it outside? I don't have anywhere in here to put it."

"No, I . . . ."

"First the golf club, then the sword. And now this. You're a regular walking hardware store, aren't you."

My tongue feels half-asleep. I try to explain, but the words come out tangled. "My stuck . . . car on the road. . . . pull this chain . . . to help somebody."

"Well, don't look at me." She brushes past me and flings the door open. "Here!" she shouts over the howl of the wind. "First drop that thing outside."

I coil the chain the best I can, then reach out and lob it onto the grass, where I hear it land with a muted clank.

She pulls the door shut, looks me up and down. "God, you are a wreck." She reaches, runs one hand through my hair, the other over my forehead. "And here, you're bleeding."

She shows me her fingers, streaked with blood.

I touch my head, where now I do feel some pain. My fingers, too, come away bloody. "How the hell . . . ?" I say.

"I don't know, Lambkin. Here, let's get you out of those clothes."

Quickly, she slips my jacket off my shoulders and yanks it by the sleeves. I watch it flop to the floor in a wet mass. I watch while she undoes my tie and drops that on the floor too.

She's going for my shirt.

"Here," I say, "I can . . ."

"No, take those shoes off, they're hopeless. We'll toss them out on the grass and let the rain wash them off."

There is no doubt about it. The woman is disrobing me. Her two wolves, their eyes bright, are watching all this intently from the corner. I can't even imagine what is going through their heads. They have that look that wolves have—a kind of no-nonsense hungry look.

Overall, something isn't right, but I'm not sure what.

Now she's unbuckling my pants.

I try grabbing her hand. "Here, wait," I say. " . . . can't my clothes off." The words don't come out right.

She slaps my hand away. "Don't be stupid, you're soaking wet. Here. Take this."

She shoves a blanket at me. Wool, it feels like. I wrap it around me, a bit clumsily. And it's only now that I realize I'm shivering. I can't stop.

"Look at you," she says.

Minutes later I'm sitting on her divan, shivering, wrapped in a blanket, otherwise stark naked. She has a wad of cotton and a bowl with some sort of amber liquid she's using to clean the cut on my forehead.

"Took a good slice out of you," she says. "Here, you want to see?"

She hands me a mirror.

She's right. It's not bleeding anymore, but there's an ugly gash just above my eyebrow.

"Could've poked your eye out."

Her bowl is gradually reddening with the blood she's cleaned from the wound.

Her wolves haven't moved, but they seem awfully close. I'm watching them eyeing me. There's not a lot of room in this gypsy wagon.

"What do you feed those wolves?"

"Nothing. Nothing at all." Her face is close to mine. She's focused on the wound. "They feed themselves."

"Right."

After awhile I stop shivering.

Grayce hands me something warm to drink. Whatever it is has a strange taste to it. She has dressed my forehead with some sort of green goop, which at the very least seems to have done no harm. The cut doesn't hurt anymore, and it has stopped bleeding.

She has wrung out my clothes and hung them by the wood stove, where they continue to drip, hissing against the hot metal. In the air currents over the stove, my shirt and my shorts stir slightly, as though dumbly alive. Hanging alongside them, one end fastened to a string, is some kind of rock crystal the size of a small cucumber, apparently a decoration. As I look around, I see the wagon is brimming with this sort of trinketry: insect carcasses, stones, bird nests, colored glass, feathers. I sit, warm and dry, listening to the storm rage outside. Now and again under the force of the wind, the wagon trembles. For the moment at least I'm happy to put off wondering what comes next.

Grayce has taken up a position kneeling at the end of the divan, peering at me intently as if watching for some sign. After several minutes of this, her expression conveys, if I'm not mistaken, a certain agitation.

"What?" I say.

She shakes her head.

She sighs. Her mouth twists as though with the force of decision, and she hops to the floor.

One of the wolves blinks.

She reaches past my shorts over the stove, and her fingers close around that crystal. Her eyes fasten again on me. Her face has taken on a different kind of expression, a little scary.

"What's that?" I say. I feel the need to say something.

"Quartz," she whispers.

She releases the crystal, spinning it with a flick of her fingers. I watch it whirl first in one direction, winding the string, then in the other. As the rotating facets spray the room with reflected candlelight, she cups her hands underneath the quartz as though catching some invisible liquid.

The effect is mesmerizing. I feel the tug of sleep, but I'm determined to keep my eye on her—though I try to be matter-of-fact about it. Whatever it is she's up to, I want to give the impression, it's her business. It makes little difference to me.

After several minutes of this, the crystal's spin is winding down. She appears finished with it. She kneels on the divan beside me.

"Michael . . . ." She pauses, reaching, caressing my hair. "I'm glad you've come."

"Me too," I try to say, but it comes out, " Mghtuf."

This brings a smile to her face.

She says, "You've undertaken a very dangerous journey."

I shrug. I'm thinking of all those downed utility poles, cars upside-down, not to mention the snakes.

She says, "I can see that you've been badly wounded."

On that point I'm about to raise an objection, but she reaches and clamps a hand over my mouth. She shakes her head.

"I'll do what I can for you," she says. "But we'll need quiet."

I nod, not wanting to contradict her. But I must say, I wasn't looking for this. She's a good soul, this girl, but I'm wondering whether my clothes might be almost dry.

She is passing her hands over my forehead in deft stroking motions. I notice also some activity about the lips, as though she's reciting something. Whatever it is she thinks she's doing, she's certainly practiced at it. I don't know where to place my eyes, so eventually I close them.

"My!" she says softly. "You have some stubbornly negative energy in there."

It's a bit one-sided, this procedure. *She* apparently is allowed to talk, while I am not. Though it's true, her voice is far more soothing, perhaps even calculated to be a part of the therapy.

When I open my eyes, I see hers are closed now. Underneath all that face jewelry, I decide, she's really not a bad-looking woman. Just, sadly, a bit of a puddinghead. She's clearly investing a lot of effort into this, though I don't feel a thing. My forehead now is slightly hot, probably because of the proximity of her hands. The main trouble is I don't know how long this is supposed to go on. When it's over, I feel, I'll have to come up with something appreciative to say. That is, if I'm allowed to speak at all.

But the minutes go by, and there's no end in sight. Despite my best efforts, I'm finding it harder and harder to resist sleep.

THERE IS the melody of a solitary bird. Somewhere. Heartbreaking in its clarion simplicity. It repeats. And repeats. I listen. Each time, I long to hear it again. But it seems the bird is not alone. Others now, just as determined, squeeze out their own songs, creating easily out of the void some weedy three-dimensionality that I cannot separate from the terrific brightness pressing me down.

I open my eyes. My head swims for a moment before I understand where I am. It is the sunlight confusing me, gushing in the windows of the wagon, sticking to everything. Sunlight. I haven't seen any sunlight for months, and now under the weight of it I feel a little slack in the muscles.

Grayce. She has vanished, and so have her wolves. I look for a note, but, as far as I can see, she hasn't left one.

As I'm standing up, my blanket slips from my shoulders and falls to the divan, where I let it lie. My clothes, still hanging over the stove, are dry. I don't put them on yet.

At my elbow, a line of Grayce's knickknacks gleam freakishly in the sun on the windowsill. I pick these up one at a time to examine them: a weathered fragment of wood, the rusted hood ornament from some extinct automobile, a scrotum-like bird's nest, a rodent skull. I'm touched. Why this trash in particular? What does it reveal about Grayce's soul that, of all the flotsam of the forest floor, she has selected these as her treasures?

I move toward the door: three or four steps and my hand is on the knob. There isn't a lot of distance to cover in here. I pause, understanding that I am naked in Grayce's wagon. I listen carefully through the singing of the birds for any other sound. I don't know whether I want to hear something or not.

Maybe Grayce is out walking her wolves.

Opening the front door, I'm hit by the full sun and at the same time by a wash of cold air. The temperature has dropped overnight—an effect, maybe, of the departing storm. Shielding my eyes from the sun, I survey for damage in the woods surrounding the meadow. There isn't a lot, as far as I can see—a few branches down here and there. Though I am struck by one spectacular change: the trees have been completely stripped of their leaves. Autumn, it appears, has come overnight.

My shoes have an inch of water in them. But, yeah, they're clean. Around them winds the chain, sparkling like some nickel-plated snake, half-buried in the grass, exactly where I tossed it yesterday. I descend to the grass, stoop, and dump the water out of my shoes, then sit down on the rusted stair of the wagon. The sun-warmed metal of the stair feels good against my bare skin. Even sitting in the sun, I'm hugging my knees against my chest, fending off the chill of the air.

While I wait, the birds go on with their singing, though it doesn't sound as soulful as before. Maybe they've grown used to their own voices. Or maybe something else. I stare and stare, but it isn't any use. I can't see them. I suppose they must be hidden in the meadow.

Mostly, though, I can't take my eyes away from the sky. That blinding blue up there, lording it over everything. Where it came from—or, more to the point, where all that drizzle and fog went—is anybody's guess. Ragged clouds are sailing past overhead, appearing and disappearing above the tops of the trees, encouraging the feeling that this remarkable sky extends beyond the meadow. Of course, I have no objective proof of that. And I'm not going to waste my time thinking about it. Sitting here calmly like this without a stitch of clothing on, my eyes half-closed in the fragrance of these weeds and grasses in the morning sun, I am content.

In my mind, a vague memory has begun to take shape. A memory, if I'm not mistaken, regarding a meadow just like this one. The memory is from a long time ago. This would have been, say, before I was born. Long before that, in fact. Something happened here, I just don't know what. But it's powerful, this memory.

"Meadow," I say out loud, "you have the advantage of me." Talking to the meadow now. Another step forward.

I look around. Everything is quiet.

There is no movement except the clouds gliding overhead.

It isn't long before I hear a branch snap, over near the edge of the woods. A large branch, it sounds like. Then I don't hear anything else.

Every hair on my body is standing straight up, each one a little antenna. I'm looking at the trees bordering the meadow. They're looking back.

After awhile—don't ask me why—I get up and clamber back into the wagon. Pulling my clothes off the line one piece at a time, I dress myself like a man preparing for his own funeral. I exit the wagon and close Grayce's charming red door and descend the stairs. The chain, it seems to me, can stay right where it is. I slip into my shoes, instantly wetting my socks, then head off down the trail toward home. If that's what I'm going to insist on calling it.

The woods seem ominously quiet. The loudest sound is the squishing of my socks in my shoes. I keep an eye out for Grayce and her wolves, but to no avail. The walk down the trail is disappointingly uneventful. In what seems like no time at all the house is there looming ahead of me.

Brenda—no surprise—is inside. When she sees me come through the back door, her eyes flare. She looks me up and down.

"What the hell happened to you?"

There is a note of extremity in her voice, though it seems more anger than worry. It's not knowing what Michael is up to, I suspect, that rankles her.

My wet shoes wheeze across the kitchen tile. The noise is so pronounced that for a moment Brenda is distracted.

"I had a little run-in with Luther," I say, flinging open the fridge door.

"Did you?" Brenda is staring at my feet.

"A little matter of fisticuffs." I rifle through a packet of swiss cheese, peel off a couple of slices. "I took a bit of a beating." I grab a can of apple juice and, with a devil-may-care flourish, elbow the fridge door closed.

"What are you talking about?"

I'm laughing while I'm telling her. "Well, first the wind knocked me flat in the parking lot. Then, after I saw that gas station rolling down the street, the highway decided to take a turn underwater. Then I skidded off the road into a ditch. And, finally, tramping through the woods to get help, I was attacked by a pack of trees." I point to the wound on my forehead. "Here. I've got the scars to prove it."

I fold the cheese, bite off half of it.

"Mm," I say, my mouth half-full. "And I was beset by hordes of snakes."

"What?"

"Here. Take a good look at this gash. This is what one tree did to me while another one held me down."

Brenda, squinting at my forehead, lets out a quick laugh. "Your head is damaged all right. But the trouble is on the inside, Michael, not the outside."

I watch her disappear down the hallway. Brenda, Mistress of Indifference. If I wanted a reaction out of her, I'd have to show up at the front door carrying my head in my hands.

I wander into the living room, where, swigging apple juice, I get a glimpse of myself in the mirror. And then I am in for a shock. "Wait a minute," I mutter. There is no gash on my forehead. I look more closely. There's no sign of a wound at all.

I drop onto the couch. I sit there, stunned.

"Brenda!" I holler. I'm not sure where she is.

She doesn't answer.

I yell, "There was a storm, right?"

Still no Brenda. Then from somewhere upstairs her voice filters down. "What do *you* think?"

"Well, was there?"

She might answer me, or she might not. It could go either way.

And then there is her voice again—distant, preoccupied. I hear her use the word "storm," but I don't hear what she says.

I rise and peek out the window, where the lawn is strewn with debris. My eyes pause to assess each fallen branch.

I punch in the number for Wendell Carlson's office.

To my surprise, Sonya's voice answers. I figure I must have misdialed.

"Yeah," she says, lowering her voice, "Rachel is out. So I'm manning the phone. Or maybe I should say womaning. What do you think?"

"Sure," I say. I'm waiting for her to bring up the subject of the storm. "So how did it go yesterday?"

"Oh, not so bad. Just your typical boring day, I guess. Except when the roof blew off our garage."

"Oh, really? Wow."

Through the window I see Swenson's truck pull to a stop in the driveway. The cab of the truck appears to be crowded with heads.

Sonya asks, "How about you?"

"Yeah, that's why I called. Our friend Luther borrowed my car."

"Uh-oh."

"It may be awhile before I can get it back."

"Well, don't worry," Sonya says. "There's only a skeleton crew in here anyway." There's something about Sonya's voice.

"Yeah," I say, "but . . . *You're* there. If you can make it in, then I should be able to."

"But for me it's a five-minute drive. And this morning it took me over an hour."

"Are there trees across the road?"

"There's everything across the road. Everything you can think of. It's one great big mess."

"Hm," I say.

The line is silent for a moment. Finally Sonya says, "There's a . . . ." She seems to hesitate. Then, " . . . Bye." I hear a click. The line has gone dead. When I call back, I get Rachel's voice mail.

Getting ahold of a tow truck eats up the better part of an hour. All emergency vehicles seem to be out on the road, beaver-like, cleaning up after the storm. Me, I'm stuck on the coffee table, the phone book open on my lap. I've been running down the listings in the yellow pages, trying to ignore the noise coming from the windows.

Out on the lawn, Swenson, outfitted with ear protection, is bent over a good-sized gnarly oak limb, which his chain saw is steadily reducing to tidy oak cylinders. Today he has with him a squad of what look like little Swensons, high school kids probably. Wearing their green-and-gold PARKS T-shirts, the kids are carrying off the sticks of oak, depositing them in Swenson's pickup truck, and otherwise campaigning over the lawn with rakes and black plastic bags and power blowers, turning my simple retrieval of phone numbers into an arduous mental undertaking. Now and then I move to the window and scowl out at them. But the kids, evidently, come equipped with Swenson's work etiquette—they avert their eyes from the house. Next thing I know, the lot of them will be upstairs piling on my wife.

I hear the saw rev, then idle. Swenson straightens, then moves on to the next tree limb.

Eventually, on the phone, I connect with someone named Harold, whose speech I can barely comprehend. I picture him short, heavy, his hair wooly-dark. He wears blue coveralls, the name Harold stenciled in gold over the breast pocket. What more should I expect of my imagination, under the duress of all this chain saw noise?

Harold, if I understand him, promises to deliver the car to me by some time this evening.

I barely have time to shower and change before the doorbell rings. Swenson, perhaps. But no, it's some red-haired, wiry guy in a plaid flannel shirt a couple of sizes too large. He is studying me with an expression of misgiving. Beyond him in the driveway I see my car chained down to the bed of a ramp truck. The engine of the truck has been left running.

"You Michael Bennett?" he says.

"Benson," I say, brushing past him to inspect the damage. I'm anticipating mud spatters, possibly a crunched fender skirt. But the car looks better than it has in months. The surface sparkles, as though he's just run it through a car wash.

"Gee," I say, "it looks great."

He opens the cab door, rummages behind the seat. "Yeah, she done . . . ." His words trail off into something that sounds like "goobernaught."

Harold (if that's who he is) works his way efficiently around the truck, unfastening chains.

I follow, observing.

"Odd spot," he mutters, "to be losing an automobile." He slaps a lever behind the cab solidly with the heal of his hand, and the truck bed begins slowly and noisily to incline. "Awfully odd spot."

His eyes fasten on me. He shouts over the noise of the truck. "Had yourself some kind of idea up there, or what?"

"Oh, yeah. No, I . . . ."

"In a hurricane?" He cants his head at me incredulously.

I shout, "No, I got lost. I thought that road would . . . ."

The edge of the ramp meets the asphalt with a clank.

He hits another lever with his hand. "Got yourself what, a little dope plantation?"

I laugh. "No, no, no. Nothing like that."

"That's all right. Don't worry." He winks. "I wouldn't take very much."

I laugh again, but he doesn't.

The cable behind the cab slowly unspools.

We both watch as the car creeps down the ramp onto the pavement.

"Odd though," he says.

U
NDER THE PRESENT CIRCUMSTANCES, I am not sure why I insist on showing up for work. But here I am in Argus Towers at 2:55 sharp, squinting down the throat of possibly yet another humiliation. In order to get here, I have just driven a delirious two hours and ten minutes over landscapes splattered with merchandise—what it might look like if all the nearby shopping centers had exploded. I drove slowly. The route was tangled by detours, as if the road were losing its memory.

Certain images stick in the mind. A lawnmower, brand new, dangling from telephone wires, its price tag twisting, fluttering against the blinding sky. A seagull with one wing missing, ravaging a bag of potato chips. Three bicycles affixed like Christmas ornaments to the same leafless tree. I took note of all these things, recognized them as the products of a new and terrible logic.

All of that is behind me now, though, as I pause on the carpet of the seventh floor, where the elevator has just deposited me. The hallway is perfectly quiet, but there's a snarly feel to the air, as though, without warning, something could emerge from any one of these offices to bite my head off. On the other hand, I have to admit, it does look like the same old hallway, the same old set of office suites. I relax the muscles of my face and stick my hands in my pockets. Somehow I'm moving vaguely forward.

I try Wendell Carlson's office first. And, sure enough, there is Sonya handling his calls. I greet her with a wave and a grin, happy to encounter a trusted soul. I'm wondering how she'll react to my growth of beard. But as soon as she sees me, her expression turns apprehensive. She glances uneasily toward Carlson's office door, which is closed. "Get ready for some changes," she whispers.

"Like what?" I say. My facial muscles are working so hard to relax, they feel tense.

"Stan is gone."

"Stan? What do you mean 'gone'?"

"Like gone. They fired him. Just this morning."

"Who fired him?"

With a toss of her head, she indicates Carlson's office. "And Vince Marconi too," she says. "They fired Vince."

"No," I say. "What would they do that for?"

Sonya shakes her head.

"On the day after a hurricane?" I say.

"What difference does that make?" She lowers her voice again. "Oh, and that's not all."

"What?"

The phone rings. Sonya picks it up. She listens. She says, "He's in a meeting."

I stare at the closed door to Carlson's office. Inside, I seem to hear something like the murmur of talk, though I may be imagining this.

"What about tomorrow?" Sonya says, her phone voice cheerful. "Yes . . . that'll work." As soon as she hangs up, the cheer vanishes. She gazes at the phone, shakes her head.

"So," I say, "he's in a meeting."

At that moment Carlson's office door opens, and he and Jack Folsom emerge chattily with some kid dressed in a suit. It could be Carlson's teenage son. Or Folsom's. Except for the suit.

"Michael," Carlson says. He seems surprised to see me. "Good you could make it in. Someone here you ought to meet."

I'm peering into the office, expecting someone else to emerge when he presents me with the teenager, whom he introduces as Steve. Steve Schoendienst. My new—incredible as it may seem—partner. Spiked hair and an earring. A cocky look on his face. And something else.

I'm dumbfounded. I look from Carlson to Schoendienst and back again. (The hell with Folsom.) I try to read Carlson's expression. Where is the explanation?

Finally I say, "So, Stan . . . ."

Carlson nods but won't give me eye contact. He seems to shudder, suggesting matters so unseemly as to remove them from the realm of discussion. "Unfortunate." That's all he says.

I don't know what else to do. I hold out my hand to Steve, who undertakes an appraisal of it before allowing himself to touch it. Even then, when our palms are joined, it feels not like a greeting, more like probing. There is something about the guy.

Carlson apparently hasn't noticed my beard. As far as I can tell, no one has. I rub a hand over it to make sure it's still there. It is.

There are smiles all around. Even I probably have one, don't ask me why. Carlson and Folsom are busy giving instructions to Steve, putting the finishing touches on whatever conversation they've just had inside that office. They appoint me as tour guide. I'm supposed to show Steve around, they say, take him down to Stan's office, and so on. That way, too, we can get to know each other.

I look at this Steve. He's looking at me. Somehow I feel I already know him.

Later, escorting Steve down the hall, I can see his head swivel this way and that way. He certainly seems to be taking things in—I will grant him that—studying, it looks like, the layout of the offices, the names on the doors, even the location of the fire escapes, as if all of this may be relevant to some plan. At one point he stops abruptly and, for no apparent reason, frowns at one of the walls. This teenager—a wall, for God's sake. I have to stop and wait for him.

As we ride the elevator down together in silence, I see him peering at his cell phone.

When we enter Stan's office, or what used to be Stan's office, Steve lets out an exclamatory whistle. It's obvious he doesn't think much of it. Ducking his head around one of the pipes, he says, "Guy worked out of this hole? What's he, some kind of rodent?"

"It takes a little getting used to," I say.

Steve barks out a short laugh. "I'll bet," he says.

"You could rearrange stuff," I say.

Steve gives me a look, as if I don't know what I'm talking about. "Why would I want to do that?" he says. "My office is upstairs."

"Oh?"

He glances around. "It's not going to be fun recovering what we'll need out of this mess." Pacing, sidling around a concrete pillar, he continues his inventory. Ducking under an I-beam, he says, "On second thought, maybe we don't need any of it."

That's what he says. That's his considered judgment, this Steve. Mr. Teenager.

He consults his cell phone. "Look, Mikie," he says, "before you leave, I'll need access to the full log on the ZACTRON probe. Then maybe in the morning we can get somewhere."

Mikie.

No one calls me Mikie. No one.

I say offhandedly, "You'll need a password."

"I've got one," he says, his words almost overlapping mine.

It seems there's no stopping this character. "Then you'll find it under Mr. Niceguy."

"Mr. Niceguy." It's not a question, the way he says it, though it seems to want an answer.

Well, I'm fresh out of answers. The fact is I've had more than enough of Steve. Especially here in the cramped quarters afforded by Stan's office. There is barely floor space enough in here for the two of us.

I move toward the door.

But Steve now is standing squarely in my way. He's staring at me. I don't know what he wants, but his attitude is definitely getting under my skin. One way or another, I want out of here. I'm forced to walk around him.

And it's then I remember where I've seen the guy. Of course, in the city. He was only a child back then, a simple snotty street urchin. He couldn't have been more than ten or twelve. The face has matured, but it's the same face. I'll never forget that look.

"How old are you?" I ask.

He gives me that same stare. Then he smirks, leans into me. "Heads up, Mikie," he says.

On the way home I swoop into the liquor store, without really intending to. After pacing the aisles for a minute or two, I observe my hand reaching out, my fingers closing around a quart of Canadian whiskey. I'm in the checkout line when I overhear the news: another sudden death in Brandewoode. The woman ahead of me is telling the guy at the register, whose name—according to the tag on his shirt—is Jeff. "Victim Number Three," she says. "Floyd Lombard." She says this as if she knows him.

Personally, I wouldn't know Floyd if he showed up in my bed, but I am more than a little shocked. "What did he die of?"

"Kidney attack."

I say, "What do you mean 'kidney attack'?"

"I don't know. Whatever it was went after his kidneys."

"You mean some kind of disease?"

"Yeah . . . I don't know."

I feel an unusual sensation, like a constriction inside my ribcage. But whether it's my lower heart or my upper kidney, I can't be sure. I'm feeling around, massaging it with my hand, when I notice Jeff looking at me.

He says, "You're not going to croak on me now, are you?"

"No, no," I say. "But it is strange, you know what I mean? All these deaths at once?"

Jeff hands me my change. "Stress," he says with finality. "There's been a lot of stress lately."

Out in the liquor store parking lot, I sit uneasily in the car. Leaving the bottle in the bag, I unscrew the cap. I peer out, my eyes scanning what I can see of the sky through the windshield. I swig a little of the whiskey. God, it does feel good going down. But it seems a small comfort. Whatever is up there, driving things, I know it isn't letting go. We're going to see worse before this is over. We're going to see much worse.

A death by a heart attack—or a kidney attack, if there is such a thing—as I understand it, is a death by natural causes. Then why the blue and red flashing lights swarming around the Brandewoode entry gate? Right away I get pulled over. This time by a Brandewoode Security van.

A younger guy with a severe expression, probably one of Jim's new hires, thrusts his face at my window. He doesn't say anything but points to my glove compartment. I fork over the same old paper: registration, license, insurance. They're starting to look a bit dog-eared from all the handling. He studies it all very carefully, taking time out to stare at my face, maybe because of the beard. He asks for a second photo I.D. I don't have one.

He pops the trunk, probes inside the car with his eyes, and, of course, finds the whiskey—the top of the paper bag wrinkled, the cap loose, wino-fashion.

Now I have to get out of the car. He looks me up and down, then he points to the centerline. "First forwards," he says. "Then backwards."

It's O.K. I feel up to the task, although this Guard is making me nervous, standing there with his arms folded. As if to say he doesn't have all evening. So, while something boils inside me, I go ahead and pace it off.

"Backwards," he has to remind me.

And I do that too: probably not a flawless performance, but no-nonsense—a good-faith effort, I believe. There's no immediate telling what he thinks of it. Nor what our neighbor Betty Johnson thinks as she drives by slowly, taking a gander.

Eventually the Guard hands me my documents. I'm allowed to get back in my car and wait while he punches information into some keyboard. I roll up the window. The back of the Brandewoode Security van, I can see from here, is equipped with a wire cage. Whether for dogs or for people, I wouldn't hazard a guess.

The Guard is still typing, punching it all in. Sitting here, I am becoming aware of something gradually—the infinitesimal growth of something, entirely soundless. I can actually feel the stab of the finger strokes on that keyboard, each of those strokes another stitch of detail in the criminal record of the new Michael Benson.

And what of the old Michael Benson? Where has he gone? And where is the life he assumed was his?—the wife with the long, immaculate legs, the birdsong and flowers and sweeping driveways of Brandewoode, the distant wooded landscapes and manicured green of the corridors bringing him, briefcase in hand, to Argus Towers daily and back again. And from his high, high office—that sunlit view to the sea. Where is it now?

I feel it again, what I felt the last time, the shame and the yawning emptiness. And at the same time the thrill. Yes. Here I am in the space behind this windshield. Connected to nothing. I am, even to myself now, a thorough unknown.

As I watch the Guard emerge from his van and walk toward me, I understand I am ready for anything. I see now how it can happen to people—pushed a little at a time, they can become actually dangerous. So strong within me is the will to resist, I feel I could explode. Under no circumstances will they ever get me into that cage in the back of the van. If he attempts it, this Guard, I will launch myself at his throat. If need be—yes—I will fight to the death.

As the Guard reaches my car, he motions for me to roll down my window. When I do, he hands me a yellow scrap of paper. A warning. Then he turns and walks back to his van.

Somewhere inside that van is my bottle of whiskey.

By the time I finally arrive home, most of the light has drained out of the day. Shadows have taken over the yard. The house itself, situated in that ambiguous space between day and night, looks somehow improbable. What does it suppose it's doing there, anyway, in the midst of all that shrubbery and lawn?

Inside, exhausted, I slump against the kitchen door, shutting it.

Brenda, passing through the kitchen on her way from one room to another, asks, "How did it go at work?"

This turns my head, attracts my attention, as it might had someone just thrown a newspaper on our front lawn. Not that her question calls for an answer, but, yes, it has registered. I consider telling her about Steve, but something argues against it. The rest of it—Stan, Vince—she wouldn't care anyway.

"Brenda," I say, "one of these days, you're going to have to open your eyes."

I say it after she has already left the room. But now that the words are out, I like the sound of them. My back still against the door, I reach and switch on the kitchen light. After a minute, I switch it off again.

Somehow over the next half hour, I manage to make a sandwich, open a beer, and flop into the hammock on the porch. That's the last I remember.

A warmth seems to pour out of the sky. I can't explain it. What I mean is, not all women are like Brenda. Really. I have known this, on some level, always. Although Brenda can cause me to forget such things or anyway make me not care enough to remember them. But then there are the moments like this (motoring through some countryside, chased by the sun and wind) when the rush of feelings is enough to overwhelm forgetfulness and the dark spell of Brenda is reversed, and I can look and I can see the woman seated next to me, her hands on the wheel, her smile surprising as an Italian sky, and I can know that her beauty arises from some other source entirely, a source I would want to hold in my heart forever, if only that were possible. There is so much. I know, a lot of this I am not seeing . . . And—yes, of course—I am forced to wonder why I would ever have chosen to enter a life with Brenda, who lacks purity. And by "purity" I mean purity. Nothing else. The throaty sound of the exhaust rising and falling as she shifts the gears, her hair complicated by the wind. I don't know what she has in mind as she glances, scouting out the road ahead, or whether we've hatched some destination together. Now winding left, now right. There is in the end so much to see, so little to understand . . . . . The sun still higher, we are sprawled now somewhere in the tall grass. My mouth is opening as if to speak. I want to ask her, but her fingers are speaking first, twirling a stalk of weed . . . Why, I wonder, are these things so elusive? The sun, the wind, these ancient hills, the meadows rolling to the sea. Somewhere, I can almost recall, beyond all of this there is . . . something. Drinking in her silhouette against the bright bright, feeling weak to the point of vanishing, I have to laugh, and we reach, and the ground spins away, the two of us hanging on, ascending, all entangled and combined as if to a new music. Clinging, suspended, taut as two snakes, and ascending, ascending, until we enter the white of the sun.

Sometime afterward, I see her smiling down on me. And I recognize that smile. I couldn't mistake it for any other. It's Grayce's smile.

"I was dreaming," I say.

She laughs. "No you weren't."

She is straddling me, the two of us perfectly naked in the hammock. My clothes and hers too, it looks like, are strewn all over the floor of the screen porch.

I look around.

"What are you doing in my hammock?"

"What does it look like?"

She presses closer, whispering, "I couldn't sleep. I kept picturing you soaked to the skin in your wet suit and tie. That heavy chain all wrapped around you." She nibbles at my ear.

She sits up, her face in shadow now against the brilliance of the porch light. She says, "Do you want me to leave? I will."

I reach and lock her in a bear hug, pull her back down next to me. The hammock is a little cramped, but it's pretty clear neither of us is going anywhere.

Then I notice something else. "Why is the porch light on?"

"I wanted to see you."

I understand perfectly, but I wonder who else might be able to see us.

I wonder a lot of things. I wonder how far away at this moment Brenda is in her bed. I wonder who might be up there with her now. It could be almost anybody. Steve even. In fact, if I had to put money on it, I'd say Steve seems the most probable.

After awhile I have to get up and get a couple of blankets.

Several times in the night, I am awakened by what sounds like howling in the woods outside. I raise my head and listen hard. Each time Grayce rubs my neck. She tells me not to worry about it. She tells me to go back to sleep.

Whatever Is Up There, Driving Things

HERE IN THE NEIGHBORHOOD where Michael lives, it is once again that time of day: well beyond the glow of late afternoon, sliding on into evening. Half an hour ago the sun sank behind a thin band of purple clouds, drawing the color out of things. The scene before us, though absolutely still, seems illuminated by a somehow restless light. Over and over, our eyes are drawn to shapes that disappear when we look at them and reappear again when we look away. Congregations of shadow wiggle and coalesce on the lawns. Night, it seems, is already finding openings, leaking itself into the world. A fairly large bat flitters over the road. Smudges of darkness rummage at the base of the shrubbery. The streetlights, lifeless sculptures in metal and glass, remain switched off.

We hear something—we are not sure what. The sound of a car perhaps. Indeed, at one end of Forest Drive, headlights flicker and appear from among the hedges. They approach slowly. And now from the opposite direction, the lights of a second vehicle gleam into view. The cars advance, each car holding exactly to its lane, the two destined logically at some point to pass one another.

In spite of the intrusion, the neighborhood for the moment seems quiet. Beyond the muffled engines of the two vehicles, we hear only the background trill of crickets and the distant hum of tires out on the highway. But now beginning gradually, there is also something else—something *unquiet*. At first hardly noticeable, originating from some distance, it flares, fast advancing—a sound to strangle the heart. Until at last there it is, fully amplifying the twilight—an astonishing, impossible scream riding down over the lawns and trees. As if the sky were erupting in pain. As if night had determined to arrive all at once and with violence. The shriek throws the bat into confusion. The smudges by the hedge freeze and then altogether vanish.

As the two vehicles draw closer together, the cry seems to swoop, and then just as quickly passes, leaving the sky raw as though inflamed. The car brake lights come on, their red glow reflecting off the road, the curbs, the lawns. The vehicles slow and in unison roll to a stop in their lanes, just opposite one another. At precisely the same instant, both rear driver-side doors swing open, and from one of the cars (a black Mercedes) a lone figure emerges. He barely has time to rise to his full height before ducking into the second vehicle (a police car). Despite the quick glimpse, we could not mistake the figure: the dark suit, perhaps a size too large, the broad-brimmed hat. By the interior light of the police car we would have a clear enough view of that face, but, for better or worse, we avert our eyes. It isn't that we can't stand to look. Rather it's our intuition that, the less we see, the better. Both vehicle doors close, the brake lights fall dark, the engines gently growl, and the cars slowly roll again in opposite directions, continuing on their way.

A moment later, their lights have disappeared, leaving the neighborhood more or less as we found it, though perhaps somewhat subdued. Whatever it is we have just witnessed, there is nothing here, animal or vegetable, that wants any part in it.

I **WAKE UP** the next morning, and Grayce is gone. So are her clothes. Every trace of her is gone. And immediately in her place I feel an ache. Flipping myself out of the hammock, I hop to the floor, as though with something definite in mind: pacing from room to room, for example, and peering out the windows, which is what I end up doing. Naked. I recognize the absurdity, this superstitious impulse to leave my clothes lying where they were when I last saw her, as if that might bring her back. But that doesn't stop me.

Out the windows, I don't see much of anything—except the usual deployment of trees, shrubs, and lawn and, once, down at the end of the driveway, a glimpse of a police car moving past on the road, slowly. A fairly typical Brandewoode morning, it would seem. Staring after the police cruiser, I run my hand over my face. My beard has a softer feel to it now, less like a wire brush. Then I'm in motion again, making my way from the living room across the hall, through the kitchen, and out onto the porch.

My God, her knees! I'm remembering. I'm staring through the screen in the direction of the back yard, though what is out there I couldn't say. I turn and retrace my steps back to the living room. Work, I decide finally. I should go to work. It might help to get my mind off her.

Upstairs I quickly shower and dress. My opening and closing of the dresser drawers causes Brenda to utter a little unconscious moan. With something almost like fondness, I watch her turn over in bed and cover her head with the pillow. I don't need to be told, it's a sight I'm not likely ever to see again.

Breakfast at the kitchen counter goes like this. Sitting on a stool, I look around at things. On the reflective surface of the toaster, a sprinkling of crumbs. At the edge of the drain board, a drinking glass, half-full of water. To my left, the refrigerator door handle. I pluck the box of corn flakes off the counter in front of me. I shake it, listen to the cereal rattle inside, as I half-suspected it would. I look around to see what else there might be, then I set the box back on the counter. And that's that. I salute the water glass before sliding off my stool. Unbreakfasted. Already I feel it in my stomach, firing away like an engine, the unmistakable sting of want.

It's when I'm passing the hallway mirror that I notice I've forgotten to comb my hair. And a minute later, when I bend to pick up my briefcase, I realize I'm not wearing socks. "Whoa," I say. I feel a tingling sensation spreading from my scalp to my limbs And a grin taking shape on my face. Probably a bearded grin.

In spite of all this, a minute later I'm standing like a trooper, my feet planted firmly on the cement floor of the garage. Why does one do things, or not do things? I have my briefcase in one hand, my keys in the other. On some level you could say I'm contemplating getting into the car. But on another level not. One thing I know, I'm paying attention to what it means to stand here. When I finally set the briefcase down, it is like relieving myself of the weight of hundreds of briefcases.

Precisely on the center of the diningroom table is a basket. There is nothing unusual about it. I'm thinking Brenda must have placed it there sometime yesterday. The basket, shaped like an upside-down hat with a handle, is piled with fruit. A few apples, pears, bananas. I pick it up. With its fruit, the basket weighs five, maybe six pounds—a good weight. But I go looking for grapes.

There are some in the fridge. When I open the fridge door, I use the chrome handle. I don't think twice about it. In among the grapes I spot a kiwi, fairly ripe. The basket is filling up, but still there's room. Cheese. What about cheese.

Heading up the path through the woods, I notice how much colder the weather has turned, compared even to yesterday. The entire floor of the forest is brightly covered with leaves knocked down by the storm, and in places I see they're coated with a milky-thin glaze of ice. As I hurry up the path, my sneakers barely making a sound, I hear skitterings and rustlings, always behind me or to the side—never where I can see. Furry little creatures, I imagine, getting ready for the winter ahead. Amazing that it comes so quickly. As for the basket, heavy with fruit and cheese, it has a good shape and a solid handle. It's no trouble to carry.

Grayce, as luck would have it, isn't in her wagon. Which, as far as I'm concerned, pretty effectively ends the day. In an instant, all that energy propelling me up the trail is gone. I wait half an hour or so out on her front step, until it begins to feel awkward. I can't sit forever. What's keeping me here is the basket. All this fruit. I'd like to be here when she sees it. I'd like to know what she thinks.

There is, however, another consideration. I can't get over the feeling I'm being observed. I understand it makes no sense. Way out here, who can see me? But the feeling doesn't go away. I end up taking just one apple. The rest I leave in the basket on the top step, where she can't miss it.

On the hike back down the trail, the air seems already warmer. The sun is easing its way in through the barren tree limbs overhead, making for an odd mix that feels like winter and summer at the same time. Increasingly there are rustlings and, in the distance now, some raucous bird noise. And other sounds. I stop. Not far away, a woodpecker—invisible to me—hammers at the trunk of a tree. I watch, alert for movement along the bark of the trees nearby. But there is no movement, only the heavy stillness drifting down slope against the sun.

The woodpecker hammers again, drawing many things together on the stitch and thread of that sound. I am ready to melt with yearning. Here, where I'd have thought there was nothing.

On impulse, I'm slowly moving again, no longer toward the house but down slope, following the air. At first I'm picking my way through ferns, clambering over rocks. Then I find a trail. The way descends and descends, then veers, traversing a slope. More and more of the trees here are evergreens—I wish I knew what kind—tall, mossy columns with boughs that block the sun. A few of the brighter leaves—red, orange, star-shaped yellow—have found their way in here. The dark needles of the evergreens capture and hold them like jewels.

The trail winds on among large boulders encrusted with a stiff, flaky vegetation that gives the rocks an ancient look. I pass along the base of a small cliff, the top of it only a few feet above my head. The cracks between the rocks are filled with wet, green moss.

And here again I stop. Something seems not quite right. I glance over my shoulder. And—sure enough—on the ledge above, a pair of wolves stand motionless, one on either side, their eyes locked onto me. I want to believe they're Grayce's, but who knows? One wolf, to me, looks pretty much like another. And if I ever doubted the size and power of these animals, I don't now. Between the two of them, if they wanted, they could tear my arms and legs off.

I look around, but no Grayce.

"Hey!" I say, as though I'm glad to have run into them, as though talking to wild animals, for me, is second nature. "Where is Grayce?"

There is not so much as a blink from either of the wolves.

Then I hear her laugh behind me. I turn, and there she is standing on a rock. My heart jumps at the sight of her.

"Hey," I say, "you snuck up on me."

She looks me up and down, grinning.

"I was just up at your wagon," I say.

She nods.

"I thought you might be there. But I . . . guess you're down here."

She squats on the rock and hugs her legs, leaving her knees to peek out from beneath her gray skirt.

"I left you some fruit," I manage to say.

The wolves seem to give their full attention to this detail.

I grope toward the cliff to steady myself.

I hear dripping. Right next to my arm, a perfect cascade of droplets is spilling from a clump of moss on the rim of the cliff. The droplets tremble and sparkle as they fall and splash to the ground, wetting my sneakers.

I seem to have lost the ability to speak.

Judging from Grayce's expression, I might be one of the funniest things she's ever laid eyes on. I don't mind. Seeing her again, it's all I've wanted since waking up this morning.

All of a sudden up in the trees there is some wild noise, like large birds fighting, eagles maybe. Or not birds. Something else.

I shoot an anxious glance overhead into the forest canopy, but what with the thick boughs of the evergreens, there isn't a lot to see.

"Hey," I say, "I wonder what that was."

"Sshh," she says. "Listen."

So I do. I stand in all earnestness, staring up into those dark boughs with my ears cocked. She watches. But it isn't long before it's clear to both of us, I'm not hearing anything.

I can easily see that I was mistaken earlier, thinking she was simple or, worse, crazy. She's not either of those things. What she is is different. A kind of different that scares me. I'm keeping a close eye on her, almost afraid to look away. Afraid that, when I look back, she might not be there.

"You know," I say, "I've been meaning to ask you something." And then I'm stuck, thinking about what that might be. "How'd you come to live all alone out here?" I say finally.

She rocks back on her heals, and her smile darkens a little.

"Don't you have any family?" I say.

Some words, right away you wish you could take them back. Grayce's smile collapses, and she looks away into the trees. But whatever it is she's seeing I don't think is there.

I feel it coming. Abruptly she stands, and the wolves leap together, one right over my head. And the next thing I know, she's gone—down the trail, the wolves running well ahead of her.

I'm not about to get left behind.

I'm running headlong—practically flying—through the woods. The patterns of light and shadow, at this speed, make it difficult to know what I'm seeing. My eyes focus on nothing in particular, somewhere just ahead of me. Impressions of the forest are blurring past. All I'd have to do is stumble over a root, and that would be the end of me, my head smashed against one of these boulders, my eyes poked out by branches. Even so, I'm not fast enough. I'm slowing down, not even sure I'm on the right path anymore. Grayce is utterly out of sight. I'm tempted to call out, yell her name. But something holds me back, some inner hardening. I understand, somehow, it would be the wrong thing to do.

Up ahead now through the trees, I think I see something. The air goes cold. I feel that first. The ground turns stony under my feet. And then—as noisy as I am—I'm aware of the silence.

Pushing past a final curtain of evergreen boughs, I blunder into an opening, where the trail ends on some rocky ledge at the shore of a great pond. I stop. I have all I can do just to stand, bent over, gasping, my hands on my knees. My lungs are on fire. Tiny pinpricks of light swarm the edge of my vision. My muscles seem to have dissolved. I want to collapse on the rock and just lie there. For some reason I don't. That vein of doggedness has taken hold, keeping me on my feet.

It's only gradually that I become aware of Grayce, sitting maybe twenty feet away. She's perched on the rock, close by the water, her back against a twisted old tree. I can see her face. Still, in spite of all the commotion I've made, she is looking, not at me, but rather out across the pond toward the opposite shore. Her body is folded into that position again, her arms hugging her legs, her knees tucked under her chin. As far as I can tell, she is perfectly oblivious to my presence. I feel like flinging myself in the water. Right there in front of her.

I remain standing like that, I don't know how long.

"Why?" I hear myself ask. I'm still out of breath. "Why'd you run away from me?"

"I don't know," she says. "It was fun."

But that's not what her face says.

I want to announce it, but it takes me a minute, as if I need to swallow something first. "I promise . . . not to do that anymore, what I did back there."

"It's O.K.," she says. "It doesn't matter."

But I don't believe her for a minute.

"I mean it," I say.

I straighten my posture, teeter for a moment, then will myself in the direction of the shore. Near Grayce I find a boulder to lean against, and, trying not to make a big deal of it, I lower myself to the rocky ground.

For a minute or two, we sit this way.

Hearing a little sound from Grayce, I turn to her. There is an unease about her presence I haven't felt before, as if something deep within her is quivering, is cold. Her fingers, clamped around her legs, are hard and white. When she speaks, her words are measured.

"I lived in a house once," she says.

I wait to hear more, but there isn't any more.

Maybe a quarter of a mile away, where she seems to be looking, the far shore drops sharply, plunging to cliffs that hang over the dull surface of the water. I've never heard anything, not so much as a whisper, about this pond, which might be big enough to be a lake. Maybe the pond has a name. Or maybe this is uncharted territory.

There is an odd feeling I can't get rid of. I glance behind us, left and right. A minute later I do it again. I say, "Do you ever have the feeling you're being watched?"

She nods. But she doesn't offer any explanation.

I nod too then. I don't know what else there is to say about it. The sky over the pond is blue, like in a painting of the sky. The few clouds drifting by overhead have a golden, wispy look to them, a little suspicious somehow. Down at eye level the surface of the pond is placid and dark, like a beautiful, terrible entrance to something.

We're both looking silently across the water. There's just a hint of expectation, as if something has already begun to happen and we're watching for the first signs of it. Without taking my eyes off that opposite shore, I fish around in my jacket pocket and bring out the apple. As I bite into it, the skin pops loudly. I'm munching away when I notice Grayce watching. I hold the apple out to her. She takes it. She looks it over, then tears a good-size bite out of it and hands it to me again. We continue sharing it that way until the apple is eaten down to the core, and the seeds fall out in my hand. I wish I'd brought another.

We sit, Grayce and I, the two of us balanced here at the water's edge. We sit for a long time, it's my impression. And I can tell, without being able to do anything about it, the place seeps into my blood. I almost forget Grayce is here.

Nearby, a tree branch is swooping low over the water. I'm looking at it. On one of its leafless twigs a single drop of liquid is suspended—maybe an ooze of sap or some melted frost leftover from the night. Now I see it quiver. Maybe a sound goes along with this. As far as I can tell, there is no wind. Shuddering, the drop hangs there low, almost touching the pond, but resisting, not giving in to the gravity of the water.

And what else? I feel a heaviness in my limbs. The air here, like some bright form of glass, makes the opposite shore unreachable as a photograph. The trees and rocks and recesses there reflect off the slick surface of the pond, just as they have reflected ever since the retreat of the glaciers.

These observations arrive like someone else's memories, like glimpses into a life not my own. I'm on the verge, partly holding myself back. In an instant, like a drop touching the surface of a pond, I could enter that life and disappear.

IT SHOULD BE late afternoon when I get back to the house. I say should because the quality of the light makes it seem like a different hour—earlier or later, I can't tell which. It feels somehow like the middle of the night in a place where there is no night.

    I don't get the chance to consult a clock. Crossing the yard, I'm stopped in my tracks by something I see down at the end of the driveway: the brake lights of a car. There, just pulling out onto Forest Drive, a black Mercedes.

    There is the raw abruptness of it, the shock, then the slithery realization that Jack Folsom has been in my home—in all probability, not for the purpose of visiting me. Curiously, whatever it is that propels me the rest of the way across the lawn, up the steps, and into the house through the back door feels more like triumph than outrage.

    Brenda is there in the kitchen, pouring a glass of soy milk.

    "Who was that?" I say.

    "Who was what?"

    I hoist myself up and sit on the counter. "That car, the Mercedes I saw leaving."

    Brenda contemplates my legs dangling in front of the cabinetry, as if they were a couple of brushstrokes in one of her paintings. But she doesn't say anything. She closes the fridge door. "Oh that. Just someone asking directions."

    I'm on the verge of laughing in her face.

    She says, "The police were here looking for you."

    "The what?"

She's been holding the glass of soy milk. She raises it now to her lips. I watch as she drinks it down. Brenda, the picture of health.

She sets the empty glass on the drain board. "The police. They want to know if you know anything about a girl living in the woods."

Her eyes have been avoiding mine, but on those last words they home in slyly. They don't let go.

I stare. "What girl?" I say finally.

Brenda ignores the question. Her eyes, locked on mine, seem to be enjoying themselves.

I say, "What the hell are you talking about?"

"*I'm* not talking about it, Michael. The police are. Anyway, you can tell *them*. They said they'd be back." She wrinkles her brow. "Is it true you left our car up there in the woods?"

"I told you, I drove into a ditch."

"What on earth were you doing up there in the first place?"

"The road was blocked, for god's sake, I was trying . . . ."

She shakes her head and turns to leave, but then pauses. "By the way, your friend, what's his name, Vance called."

"Vince? Vince called?"

Brenda, heading for the hall, is not about to elaborate.

"What did he want?"

"I don't know," her voice answers from the hall. "He said he had something to tell you." I hear her feet on the stairs.

I figure I might as well walk to Vince's place. It's only a couple of blocks. Normally I'd take the car, but I don't want to risk getting stopped by the police. On foot, if I have to, I can duck into some shrubbery. I walk with my hands buried in the pockets of my windbreaker. Michael Benson, I'm thinking, fugitive from justice. Then I hear myself actually say it. "Michael Benson, fugitive from justice." Each word puffs out as breath, then tatters and disappears into the cold. The temperature has been plunging again. Those wispy clouds of this morning have taken on thicker, darker shapes, muscling out the sun. And the wind is picking up. I know it's impossible, but it feels like winter. Something in the air makes me anxious to see Vince. I wonder what he wants to tell me.

I'm nearing a recess in the Renshaws' hedges when I pass through the unmistakable odor of cigarette smoke. I turn, and there—not five feet away, standing amidst the myrtle—is the most desperately disheveled woman I've ever laid eyes on. Her skirt and jacket are stained and torn. Her gray hair, wildly tangled, holds twigs and bits of leaves. What are left of her stockings are down around her ankles.

This is something new. I have heard about homeless people, of course, but I've never actually seen one. Not this close up. Not in Brandewoode.

Though her head is turned slightly to the side, the poor woman is watching me warily. Drawn in by those sad, terrified eyes, I find her both repulsive and at the same time oddly touching. Her hand inches up, bringing a crooked cigarette to her mouth. Hungrily she sucks a drag down, holds it, then exhales, emitting along with the smoke a husky little moan. There's something about the smell of that smoke.

I step closer, wanting a better view of her, though still careful to keep a safe distance. She has an unpredictable look about her. As I move in, the woman ducks defensively, shrinking, as though expecting me to strike her.

"Don't worry," I say. "I'm not going to hurt you."

She moans again, studies me curiously.

The voice of that moan sounds somehow familiar. I say, "Do I know you?"

She leans a little forward, squinting at me. "You?" she says, her voice hoarse. "Are you Benson?"

I can't believe my ears. "Marjorie?" I say. "Marjorie Lundstrom?"

"Oh," she says. "Oh. Thank God." She slumps, sagging against the hedge until at last she's sitting on the ground. Stiff twigs and leaves are raking the snarl of her hair. The poor woman looks positively grotesque.

"What happened?" I say.

She shakes her head. Her fingers play with the leaves of the hedge. She seems to whimper. Her breathing is ragged. I'd be tempted to take that cigarette out of her hand, but I don't dare touch her. Who knows what could be wrong with her?

Her voice begins a weak, high-pitched whining, in which gradually I recognize words.

"God," she whines. "Oh, God. I can't believe it."

"What?" I say.

She breaks off, whining again and blathering. If only she'd pull herself together long enough to tell me what's wrong. Finally amidst the puling and moaning, I begin to hear actual words again. But the poor woman is incoherent. I can barely understand her.

"... almost had me ... Lord, God ... they came this close ...." She holds her finger and thumb a millimeter apart.

"Who?" I say.

"Figured they'd done it!" She drags deeply on her cigarette. "Poor old Marge, right on the end of their fork."

I give up hoping to get sense out of her. I try just to calm her down.

"That's too bad," I say. "That's awful ...."

Her words are gravelly again, that old familiar voice. "Christ, Benson, but I got clear of them. Clean away." She cackles.

I'm nodding. It isn't easy pretending this is an actual conversation. Leaning out to the curb, I check both ways, up and down Forest Drive. I don't want any more surprises.

Marjorie grabs ahold of the hedge and pulls herself to her feet. She brushes at her skirt, runs a hand over her hair. "I'm a mess, I know." She flicks her cigarette butt. It lands in a clump of dead leaves caught at the base of the hedge. After all that talk about fire, I'm about to warn her when suddenly she snatches my wrist, tugs me in close. She says, "I'm sorry, Benson. I shouldn't have treated you the way I did. I don't know what I could have been thinking."

"Oh, I wouldn't worry ...."

"Look," she says. She's squeezing my wrist hard. "My advice to you, sweetie, you get yourself out of here. Now. And don't think I'm fooling. You don't know what you're up against. These people, there isn't a thing they don't know about you. God, the number of syllables on your great-grandmother's tombstone. Believe me, they have it, in a file somewhere. They can listen in the dark while you tie your shoelaces and, by the sound alone, know that it's you and no one else. Silicon, honey. They've got you mapped up, down, and sideways. Every last synapse, every last scrap of protein, your own personal devils with their fingers on the keyboard. You go. You get yourself clear of them. And not that way, either." She yanks me away from the curb. "All the roads are covered. They're watching the streets like crows. Cross-country, dear. It's the only way. Come on."

She turns, letting go of my wrist, and plows straight into the hedge. Its branches are stiff, unyielding. They bounce her right back. She lowers her head and inserts herself again. I watch the poor woman flailing, struggling, getting nowhere. I can hear her skirt tear further. But she wriggles and thrusts and claws her way, and after a minute, amazingly, she makes it through. I can't see her anymore.

For several minutes I'm just standing there. I can't decide. Marjorie's warning about the roads has given me second thoughts, but there's no way I'm following the woman through that hedge. I check once more up and down Forest Drive. Seeing the street deserted, I set out at a trot for Vince's place.

It doesn't take me long. At the corner of his yard I duck into a clump of shrubbery and drop to my knees. And for awhile I just stay put that way. It seems I need for once to catch up to myself, to take a solid measure of my surroundings. Breathing heavily, kneeling there in the bark mulch, I peek out from under the bushes, at the yard and at Forest Drive. It strikes me as odd that the street is so quiet. And for that matter, so are the properties themselves. It is as if the houses and yards have been here like this always. Empty. As if there have never been any people. As if there has never been the need.

After a few more minutes of this silence I think I hear a sound. I can't tell what it is. I'm straining, listening, but the harder I try, the less certain I am that I hear anything. Tentatively I get to my feet, thankful now for Vince's elaborate landscaping—here a curlicue of garden, there a flourish of shrubbery. Just a few days ago this yard would have been picture-perfect, not a leaf or a blade of grass out of place. Now, I have to say, it's a bit of a mess—all Vince's hard work, storm-battered and browned by frost. Still there are plenty of places to hide.

I've just started across the lawn, moving in the direction I thought the sound came from, when—it figures—I hear a car engine. Lunging, I hit the ground behind a double row of red-blossomed cannas. Or at least they used to have red blossoms. Peering out from between their thick, purplish stalks, I just get a glimpse of a Brandewoode security van crawling past before it disappears behind a line of bushes. I keep my head down and listen. The engine doesn't slow or speed up but continues, steadily receding, until I can't hear it anymore. But this time I'm not taking any chances. I wait.

I'm lying, contemplating the shriveled canna petals that litter the bark mulch—all those sad, disintegrated flowers just inches from my face—when I hear the noise again. It seems to be coming from behind the house, which is the direction I'm headed anyway—the front door is too exposed. The noise is faint, weirdly metallic. I get a whiff of smoke too, as if somebody's burning leaves.

Crouching low, mostly out of sight, I work my way further along to where I have a view of the back yard. Everything looks peaceful. It's clear, whatever is causing the noise is inside the walled semi-enclosure of the courtyard, where just weeks ago I sat with Vince, sipping those gin-and-tonics.

And there! Just over the courtyard wall now, I notice movement among the branches of Vince's apple trees—the predatory-looking business end of a pole saw. Of course. It's Vince, pruning his trees. The wall has a little Mediterranean-style window built into it. A couple of steps to the left and I can see the man himself framed in the window.

I call, "Hey, Vince!"

He looks over, gives me a puzzled squint, and finally nods. Then his expression changes. I don't know why.

I lose sight of him as I'm moving around to the courtyard entrance. Then, god!—the moment explodes. Out of nowhere—I hear him scream. As if he'd just lopped his own finger off with the nippers.

"Ho, Vince!" I yell.

But his screams turn to a sound far worse, mixed in with some gurgling noise. It's awful to hear.

I'm running, but I feel I'm never going to get around that wall. Finally I reach the entrance, in time to see the pole saw where Vince must have dropped it—or flung it—still sliding against the wall, then clattering onto the flagstones at my feet. There is Vince on the ground, though he's not the same Vince, but a Vince that something has happened to. He's lying on his back, his face the color of liver, his body jerking convulsively, his eyes fixed crazily upward, where for some reason I don't want to look. But I do anyway. And then I see it, or almost see it—some emaciated replica of the sky, sliding away as if on a string, leaving in its place this glowering lavender, these collusive clouds. And it seems to have taken the air with it.

It's as if my voice comes from outside of me. "Vince," it moans, " . . . Vince."

Then a noise, a door slamming somewhere. Poking my head through that window in the garden wall, I see a man in a dark suit hurrying down the front walk. I don't know whether it's one of the neighbors or maybe some salesman.

I let out a yell, "Help! Hey there! We need help here!"

But the guy, I don't know whether he's stone deaf, or just one of these people who doesn't want to get involved. He just keeps on going, one hand holding onto his damned hat. He's practically sprinting now out to the road, where I lose sight of him behind the hedges.

I scream with all the power in my lungs, "Bastard! You bastard!"

The air's so electric, my hands are shaking. I can't believe the guy wouldn't stop.

"That's the trouble with this goddamned neighborhood," I say. "Always everyone for himself!"

As for Vince, it's over for him. He shudders once, then lies absolutely stone still on the patio, his head in the nasturtiums.

Vince, my good friend—seconds ago he was here. Now gone. Swarming pinpricks of light—I'm trying to see through them. I'm stumbling, not sure where my feet are anymore. It feels the way it feels in dreams, when you're trying to do something and your body refuses to move. I wonder, is this the way it started with Vince? I can feel it in my marrow, spreading. A kind of impotence. A kind of paralysis. I'm thinking, so this is what it's like. The end, so quick. So unprepared for.

Somehow I pick up the pole saw. It's there in my hands. I'm backing out onto the lawn beyond the courtyard, sweeping one way and then the other with the thing, expecting . . . I don't know what. Anything. Anything! Finally I'm just standing there, shaking. Looking down, I see my fingers, dead white, gripping the pole saw. But I can't feel them. I take a step, then another, edging toward the neighboring property, back toward the direction I came from. In the distance I hear a siren. I'm aware again of smoke—somewhere there's a fire.

What else is there to do but turn and run over the grass like a madman, pole saw in hand. I don't even know why I'm running. Not to get help for Vince—a guy who is beyond help if anyone ever was.

Happily, the adjacent back yard—I think it's the DiSilvias' property—is nothing but open lawn. It gives me a pretty clear field of view all the way to the woods—though I must say the scene has an ominous look to it. Swenson, I guess, hasn't gotten around to this neighborhood yet. Not only is the ground still littered with leaves and debris from the storm. It's also alive with snakes. I really have to watch my step. And there's the smoke—more of it now. I cross over into the next yard, which is open also. Then, to get my bearings, I cut back out toward the street. And there I really get a shock. I understand now where the smoke is coming from. A good part of the Stengels' front yard is on fire. And that's not all. Moving past the corner of the house, I can see, across the street, the Renshaws' hedge is all ablaze. The flames must reach twenty feet high. The fire has taken over several lots and is spreading.

This wet ground? Could this all have ignited from Marjorie Lundstrom's cigarette? Incredible. I should have said something to her. I'm hurdling the line of flames on the Stengel's lawn and running along the curb opposite the Renshaws' hedge. Suddenly out of Linden, a couple of blocks away, a fire truck swings into view, and right behind it a police car. Both, at the same time, cut loose with their sirens. I dive behind the only cover available, the smoking remains of some shrubbery bordering the Stengels' driveway. The fire truck, approaching, sounds like five fire trucks. I hear it squeal to a stop right in front of me. Doors are slamming, firemen yelling. That burning hedge roaring like a waterfall.

I make my way, crawling, along the line of shrubs, propelling myself on my elbows military fashion, dragging the pole saw by its rope. Even this far away I can feel the heat from the fire across the road. The smoky air is flickering red and blue and red in berserk rhythms. The ground underneath me is charred and wet. I'm really careful about not being seen, but it probably doesn't matter. The firemen, the cops—they're all too busy with the fire, yelling, unspooling their hoses, hustling around. They've got a hydrant a half a block away. They go to work on that.

Near the corner of the Stengels' house, I judge it's finally safe to stand. My pants, jacket, sneakers—all are smeared with a wet charcoal grime. The same with my hands and—I see reflected in one of the windows—my face. I look like something that's just wriggled its way out of hell. I give the scene one last glance over my shoulder. The fire seems, if anything, worse. And all those yellow raincoats. Like hornets.

I work my way back cautiously along the side of the house, carrying the pole saw like a spear. I don't know what I'm going to do with the thing, but there is comfort having my hands on something that feels like a weapon. Skirting the air conditioner, I turn to cross through the back yard, what I probably should have done in the first place.

About midway through the yard I happen to look up, and there, standing in the floor-to-ceiling window, is Gloria Stengel. My hand naturally goes up to wave, though the look on her face is one, not of friendly recognition, but rather of horror. The lawn behind me is empty. It's me she's reacting to, her lips moving now, as if she's trying to say something. Then I notice she has a cell phone—the last thing I need.

I'm shaking my head, waving my arms. "For God's sake, Gloria," I yell. "It's me! Michael!" I take a step toward the window. But, her face gripped by panic, she slips out of sight behind the curtain. For an instant I stand there, nodding, comprehending fully and as if for the first time the twisted logic of things. I'm remembering, too, what Brenda said. The police want to question me. They want to know about a girl living in the woods.

I don't know what separates that moment from the next. But at some point I'm running. I don't look back.

THE BRANCHES of the trees overhead are clacking in the dark. But there's another sound, a new sound. As soon as I stopped to get my bearings, I heard it. The sound isn't actually coming from the trees, but from beyond, it seems, possibly from far away. Maybe it has to do with the wind, or with the arrival of something. Like the National Guard. Or a pandemic. Or legions of flying things never seen before. I'm not excluding any of it.

I imagined the night would be black as ink. But it isn't anything like that. Every twig, every flake of bark, every spent leaf and stone on the forest floor is throbbing slowly orange. Weird—as if an immense and final sun is steadily gathering itself, preparing to lift, just once, above the western horizon. It's the fire raging all across Brandewoode, spilling its unsteady glow even here. Also now the smoke is moving in, finding its way by trial and error, sniffing around the moss-covered logs and boulders, alert for openings.

From where I squat hunkered down among these rocks, the only direction, it seems, is up. In the smoldering light, the trunks of the trees ascend like the walls and pillars of some fire-lit cavern. Lying low, lizard-like in my charcoal clothes, my fingers splayed against the rock, I seem to fit right in. Still, I am cautious. Maybe there are snakes here, maybe there aren't. That faraway noise is fading, now rising, now fading again. Like a male chorus howling out some chant, without words. Or, if there are words, they're in a foreign language. One I've never heard before. Echoing and filtering in through the trees as though the forest itself were moaning.

    I don't stay put for long. Before I know it, I'm on the move again, hurrying through the underbrush, skirting boulders, hurdling logs. There are times when one thing or another—some noise, some lurch of shadow—causes me to grip the pole saw with both hands, maneuvering it at the ready. But mostly it stays at my side. I'm beginning to like the feel of it there, balancing on the cradle of my fingers. The cord is gathered in a coil and tied off just in case. As I walk, I see the dull glint of the saw blade ahead of me slicing through the ferns and other vegetation like a shark fin. My stride is determined, elastic, fed by an energy unfamiliar to me. Something is driving me—not vengeance, not fear, but something. There is only one place I need to go. Even as I'm thinking about it, I run across the trail. I veer onto it, heading up slope, cutting through orange-tinted lenses of smoke hanging thick above the forest floor. Their remnants fly apart and swirl as I pass.

    And now up ahead, complicating the glow, flashes of red and blue splatter the edges of the tree trunks, and there are fresh rufflings of noise. Crouching, melting into the woods, I steal through the brush roughly parallel with the trail. There's a change in the air. Sounds are larger, coming at me now horizontally. I know the edge of the meadow is just ahead.

    I'm drawn to an opening in the wall of brush, where light is coming through. It gives me a good view of the meadow. There, looming out of the tall grasses, are a couple of police SUVs, doors flung open, emergency lights whirling like helicopter blades. In the glare of their headlights, Grayce's wagon, the near corner of the meadow, the smoke roiling from the woods—all are as plain as in full daylight. Both engines are running. The radios crackle on and off with what sounds like gibberish—vehicles talking to one another in the language of machines with wheels.

    Voices are coming from Grayce's wagon, which is lit up inside as though every lantern in the place is cranked up high as it will go. I see two men, I'm guessing plainclothes detectives, one of them rummaging through the place, the other standing over her. Now and again one or the other says something, but I can't hear over the noise of the SUVs. And there are other, more distant sounds—what might be explosions. I am distracted, too, by the pure spectacle: the dire, smoldering glow of this space hollowed out of the forest, the insane clamor of the colored lights. Great sinews of smoke emerge from among the trees and twist, sliding over the meadow. I watch them, openmouthed. And at the center of it all is the enigma of those silhouetted figures in the bright windows of Grayce's fairy-tale wagon. There is, I understand, an ominous beauty about the world.

"What is all this shit?" one of the men yells.

I hear a crash.

Grayce says something. I can't make it out. She doesn't sound happy.

A uniformed police officer is standing outside by the steps, his attention apparently divided between the meadow and what's going on inside the wagon. He's eating something. An apple—from my basket of fruit! He keeps peering into the smoky dark behind the vehicles, where I see shadowy movement, as though things are prowling around out there. Maybe he sees this too.

Crouching, I'm taking it all in. Then my eyes settle on those two SUVs. I feel on the verge of an idea, if you can call it an idea. It's more like an urge that begins in my fingertips—the rest of me simply follows the lead. So it's almost a surprise to find myself now duckwalking from the cover of the woods out into the meadow, pole saw and all. The grass is tall enough to hide me from view as I scramble, staying clear of the headlights. At the first rear tire, I stop. The tire is oversized, clotted with mud. My fingers get to work, unscrewing the valve cap and poking the valve open. I muffle the escaping air with my jacket, but it probably isn't necessary. There is so much noise as it is. I don't let all the air out, only some of it. If the vehicle settles crookedly, it might arouse suspicion. I work my way around to the other tire and open that one up. It takes awhile, back and forth between the two tires, before they're both perfectly flat. Inside the wagon, meanwhile, the talk goes on sporadically.

I'm moving on to the second vehicle when I put my hand down on something wriggly. A goddamned snake! I jump back, give a little yelp, and immediately regret it. Sitting on my heels, flat against the bumper, I watch the snake wriggle off through the weeds.

The voices in the wagon fall silent. Then one of the detectives says my name. ". . . something something Michael Benson . . ." is what I hear.

I freeze. I wait, wondering whether they heard me, wondering whether right now they're circling the vehicle, guns drawn. I hold absolutely still.

Nothing happens.

". . . something something fucking arsonist," one of the voices says.

Then the door to the wagon bangs open. I hear shoes on the metal steps.

I lean, peering around the SUV bumper to where I can see what's going on.

They're all out on the grass. I can hear their voices better now.

"Come on, sugar," one of them says. "My colleague here is losing his patience."

Grayce doesn't say anything.

I can't quite see her. Maybe she shrugs or makes a face. But my view of her is blocked by the front fender.

The other detective says, "Waste of time, Frank." He kicks at the grass, gazes up into the night. "We ought to torch this hen house and be done with it."

Frank shakes his head, stares down at his shoes. He turns, hands on his hips, and surveys Grayce's wagon. He gives it a long appraising look, like someone deciding whether to buy it. "Well, Billy, it would be a shame. I like the girl. Fundamentally, I think she's a good sport. I think her heart's in the right place. She just doesn't like to be rushed."

"No kidding," Billy says.

There is something about their voices I don't like.

Frank is looking straight at Grayce. He says, "People want to live lives of quiet independence, out here in the woods like this, they have a perfect right. It's not our job to pass judgment."

Billy's cell phone rings. He answers. "Yeah? Yeah. Why not? No. No." He glances at Frank. "Fuckin wild goose chase. Yeah. Sure. I'll tell him." He clicks his phone shut, nods at Frank.

The smoke is thickening, drifting in front of the headlights, casting eerie shadows over the scene.

"Well, Billy," Frank says, "maybe you've got a point." His voice has a new edge to it.

"I told you," Billy says. Now he's staring at Grayce. "There's no getting through to this broad."

"No. You've got a point."

"I mean, look at her face, for Christ sake." Billy seems to be warming up now, gathering steam. "Looks like she had reconstructive surgery at a friggin tinsmith's." He laughs.

I lean out further to where I can see Grayce.

I see him reach and lift her chin with a single finger. "Hey, guess what, honey, you're rivets are showing." He laughs. Frank chuckles too, shakes his head. The uniformed cop shifts his feet—he grins but he doesn't say anything.

All of this is illuminated brilliantly by the headlights.

Suddenly Billy yells out, "Ow, Christ! She bit me, the little bitch!" He grabs her, slaps her. "I'll have to get a fucking tetanus shot now."

She wiggles free, but they catch up to her. The two of them have their hands on her. All this seems to be happening all at once.

And not only that. Something else is happening too. I am. Like an explosion. Like a comet, hurtling out from behind the SUV. In a fury. I am twelve times my own size. I am weightless. Thoughtless. I'm charging, swinging the pole saw in a great swath. In no time, I'm into the headlights—I feel it like a wash of energy. My mouth flies open and, as I'm bearing down on them, all the rage inside me rushes out in a lion's roar. "GAAAAAAHHHH!!" An absurd cry, really. But for an instant, jaws dropped, they're all just staring at me. Like witnesses to the gates of hell thrown open.

The pole saw catches Frank square in his back, knocking him into the weeds.

"What the fuck!" Billy screams, lurching back, off-balance.

The uniformed cop, reaching for his gun, trips over the stairs to the wagon. His gun tumbles into the grass. All of this seems to happen at once, and I see it. And I see, at the same time, that Grayce is gone. She disappears so quickly.

The cop by the stairs is lunging for his gun now.

I turn and run.

"Jesus fucking snake!" It's the uniformed cop yelling, his voice high-pitched, almost girlish. "I went for my gun, Jesus, I picked up a goddamned snake!"

" . . . was him!" This is Billy's voice now, receding.

Frank screams something.

Billy yells, " . . . was fucking Benson."

I'm running. Out of the meadow and into the woods.

There's yelling behind me. I hear a gun shot. Then a second. I keep moving. I almost can't hear their voices now. I'm threading my way among the trees.

Glancing behind, I can't see the lights of the vehicles. I slow down. I stop. I have no idea what direction I've taken, or whether I've been running in a straight line. All around me, vaguely outlined in orange, the trunks of the trees rise into the night, up and up, until at some point they disappear in darkness. Wherever their branches are, I can't see them. I'm crouched next to a rock. I'm listening carefully, trying to pick out sounds. The only thing I hear is my breathing. It gives me a strange feeling, as though I could be the only living thing left in the world.

"O.K., Benson," I whisper, "now what?"

"Keep still," a soft voice says. Grayce's voice.

I turn, and I can see her, maybe five feet away. "Holy . . ." I say. "How'd you find me?"

She puts a finger to her lips. Tinged with orange like the trees, her eyes bright, she looks like a spirit born of embers.

We wait, listening.

She says, "That was an impressive rescue."

"Oh. Thanks."

"What was that you hit him with?"

I'm holding the fiberglass shaft vertically like a spear, leaning on it. "Pole saw," I say.

Her eyes travel the length of it up to the blade. There is genuine admiration in her expression. She says, "You're something else."

We're waiting there, the two of us. I'm looking all around me at the tree trunks, the rocks. The smoke seeking its way up the forest floor and down, like something with intention. Everything orange, everything pulsing, none of it holding still. None of it content with the way things are. I've already taken out my little notebook. By the ocher light, I'm jotting things down. Impressions. Ideas. At one point I glance over. Grayce is watching, her eyes on my pencil hand.

Soon, vaguely from the direction of the meadow, a dull flash illuminates the spaces between the trees, as if someone has turned on a fluorescent light. We hear a soft concussion.

Grayce says, "There goes my place."

Then distantly the lights of a single vehicle are moving, flickering ghostlike through the forest. The vehicle seems to stop, then go again. We watch until it disappears.

Grayce stands up, hands something over to me. A knapsack. We stare at each other.

I can feel the woods around us fading, succumbing to the throb of that terrible loveliness. And it's immediately clear. This chapter is finished. Frank, Billy, the rest of them, they'll be back with dogs, and worse. If they catch us, they'll eat us alive. It will never be the same here.

"O.K.," I say, "but where are we going?"

She looks around as though she hasn't decided.

I have a sudden undeniable urge. "Let's go this way," I say, pointing.

We walk on and on through the night, keeping up a good pace. Grayce seems to know her way around these woods, finding one trail after another. She doesn't stick with one very long before veering onto the next. But often enough, when we come to a junction, that powerful urge reawakens in me, pulling in one direction or the other. And then she defers to me. I don't know where the feeling comes from, but it's so strong, I don't question it. The trouble is, increasingly mixed in with this is another urge, one that I'm more doubtful of, one that I suspect is unhealthy. It's the desire to see Brenda again, or rather for her to see me, with Grayce. It's hard for me to separate these two forces, to know which one is drawing me one way and which the other. To all of this, Grayce seems oblivious. She is paying attention to local things: the direction in which the trees are leaning, the condition of their bark, the sound and feel of the leaves underfoot.

Urges or no urges, I soon lose all track of where we are. Once or twice, without making a big deal of it, I throw a glance back at Grace, but it's impossible to tell what she's thinking. The way we're going, the smoke seems to be thinning. I can breathe better. So I guess we're heading away from the fire. And it's getting colder. Little by little the orange glow fades, which makes it harder to see. It feels as if we're journeying into night itself. Still, somehow in all this blackness things retain a kind of visibility—accessible, not to the eyes exactly, but to something.

Early on we hear a couple of distant explosions. For the rest of the night, helicopters are thundering back and forth overhead at intervals, sweeping the forest with searchlights. At one point one of them, maybe catching sight of us, circles back and descends. We duck among the rocks and ferns. Clutching at tree roots, we press ourselves flat against the ground. Through the bare branches of the trees, we feel its lights, hot and brilliant as any lowering sun. We're holding on in that momentless space just before the bullets hit with certainty, sewing us to the earth. The helicopter hovers that way, then drifts off.

We get right up, and we're walking again. I should be tired, but I'm not. There is a bit of a breeze and a nip to the air. We open up the packs and put on warmer clothes—sweaters, neck warmers, woolen caps, she's brought it all. There's water, and food too—a bread with a kind of seed in it, and some soft cheesy stuff. I don't ask Grayce what it is. We walk while we're eating.

But it isn't long, and—we both notice it—things are turning orange again. The smoke is denser too. It's as if we've taken a wrong turn and are heading back toward the fire. These urges of mine, after all, what do I know about them? A lot of good it will do to have Brenda witness Grayce and me being broiled to death. We turn and turn again, each time away from the advancing glow. But soon enough we feel the heat again: somehow the fire is gaining on us.

Stopping at a trail junction, we're surprised: in spite of the thickening smoke, we can see each other's faces. We understand, dawn is breaking. And this too: seeing Grayce sagging against a tree, I realize I am exhausted. We can't keep going much longer. We look at each other. Following one last urge, I turn left.

We hurry on along the trail for what, ten minutes? twenty? forty-five? Time fades in and out of the smoke, the heat driving at our backs. Eventually, up ahead, I see something through the trees that looks like water. It could be the pond. If we waded into it, I'm thinking, maybe we could survive the fire that way. But when we break out onto the rocky shoreline, we get a bit of a jolt: there is nothing, nothing but water, as far as I can see. We've come to the shore of the bay. Ice is already forming along the edges. Further out, the water looks a bit rough, speckled with whitecaps, or maybe chunks of ice. The sky just above the horizon has taken on a yellow glow, but clouds are moving in from the west, and it's beginning to spit snow.

Meanwhile, tendrils of smoke now are issuing from among the trees along the shore, probing, getting their bearings. It won't take long for them to find us. Again Grayce and I look at one another. There's nothing to say.

We head east, slipping and stumbling along the shore. The rocks and the skim of ice slow us down. Smoke and cold wind. Fire and ice. We're threading our way in between. It looks to me like the end for us, until the idea hits me. And from then on, I have only one thing in mind. Stan's boat.

When we arrive at the wharf, it's maybe nine o'clock in the morning. Not that there's such a thing as time anymore. I worried that we might attract too much attention, wearing the clothes Grayce packed for us, these oversize rustic woolens in muted tones. But we don't see a soul, not so much as a stray dog. Around the wharf there's not even a rowboat left in the water. My heart sinks when I realize, Stan's boat is gone too.

I walk right to the end of the pier and stand, the toes of my shoes jutting over the edge. I look out toward the horizon, that zone where the sky meets the sea and where, like it or not, boats disappear. I'm staring hard, purposefully, as if the undeniable purity of my will could influence that boat of Stan's, could arrest it and call it back.

"Stan," I whisper. I put my heart into it, so that it comes out sounding like a prayer.

"That you, Michael?"

I can actually hear his voice. But behind me. I turn and there he is. I'm not a hugging sort of guy, but I come pretty close to grabbing him right there, except that he has his arms wrapped around a couple of canvas bags. And I'm a little awkward with my pole saw, holding it like a goat herder's staff.

Stan is staring at the pole saw, looking it up and down, his mouth twisted into that bent smile of his. He says, "What are you fitted out for?"

"Oh," I say, "it's a long story."

"What the hell happened to your face?"

"Aw . . ." I shrug. "I was trying to put out the fire."

He just looks at me.

"This is Grayce," I say, pointing. "Spelled with a Y," I add, maybe thinking to impress him.

He nods and Grayce nods, the two of them sizing each other up. But, I can tell already, not like with Brenda. Nobody's fur is up.

"I was afraid we were too late," I say.

"Another two and a half minutes, and you would have been. Come on, we're around the other side of the quay."

We've been aboard barely two minutes when I hear the engine start. Stan casts off from the wharf. We're underway in no time, sliding out into the bay, Dolores at the helm, the wind tearing away at her green hair. Standing over against the rail, I feel I should be doing something, but I don't know what. The decks have all been cleared. My pole saw, that was first to go, stashed away down below somewhere. Dolores wouldn't have it anywhere near the rigging. My fingers probe in my back pants pocket. I can feel it there, my little notebook.

I look back at what we're leaving behind. All along the rocky shore, dark smoke is pouring out from between the trees. And now, behind those trees, we see what we couldn't see before, the flames advancing like armies. A hundred yards off shore we still feel the heat. Damn Marjorie Lundstrom's cigarette! But it's too late now.

Grayce doesn't look at the fire. She's up there in the bow, hanging onto the rigging, staring straight at the horizon ahead, like someone under the spell of the future. Or maybe she's thinking about her wolves. I remember what Swenson said, about the forest surviving, and I think of telling her this. But then I wonder, maybe she already knows.

All at once the engine falls silent. Not a good sign. But Stan explains, we're taking the tide out. And the wind's behind us.

Dolores is shouting orders now. Hoist this, feather that. Stan translates. Grayce and I hesitate, clipping and unclipping hardware. We haul on ropes. Sometimes I do the wrong things. Grayce makes mistakes too, laughing into the wind. A sail unfurls, then another. We're not very good at it yet, but slowly the ship undergoes a change. You can feel it being pulled through the water, as if by the hand of God.

The temperature continues to drop. If it keeps up like this, Stan says, the ice will build on the hull. If that bothers Dolores, you couldn't tell by looking at her.

It isn't long before land is just a thin, dark band on the western horizon. The sky above it is the color and texture of asphalt. Off to the left, I can see it, standing taller than anything else, Argus Towers, flames now lapping at the base of it. Stan's watching it too. "Hah!" he says, his fist in the air.

We're out on the ocean now. At sea. Who knows where we're headed. These waves are getting pretty heavy. Grayce is looking at me. I've never seen a woman so beautiful. I'm thinking. Heroism. I guess, under the right circumstances, it is still possible. All that waiting around in between. That's the hard part.

mafic
g

PORTLAND PUBLIC LIBRARY SYSTEM
5 MONUMENT SQUARE
PORTLAND, ME 04101

WITHDRAWN